The Siren's Gentleman

Fate of the Worthingtons

Laura A. Barnes

To William:
Thank you for helping me see the vision I had for this series &
encouraging me to keep trudging along through every obstacle
I came upon

The Siren's Gentleman

Chapter One

G RAHAM RUSHED ALONG THE hallway, the flickering candles in the scones only offering him a small amount of light in his endless pursuit. He followed the white billowing skirts trailing behind the mysterious figure who was always within his reach, yet unable to be grasped. She haunted his dreams, consumed his every waking moment, but he held no clue about who she might be. Even now he couldn't call her name and beg for her to wait for him. Because without a name, she would forever be a figment of his imagination.

She led him along one hallway after another, teasing him with a glance of her features when she looked over her shoulder to see if he still followed her.

"Stop," Graham yelled, but she responded by running away. The farther she ran, the more the shadows following them closed in, suffocating him with their heaviness.

Graham rounded the corner and came to a halt. She had stopped on the edge of the decaying house. Strong winds whipped the air, lifting the locks of her raven hair to swirl around her, and the layers of her skirts slapped against her legs in a billowing haze. The girl slowly turned, and once again Graham stood speechless at her exquisite beauty. There were no words to articulate the beauty he gazed upon.

Lightning slashed as the sky opened up to pelt them with harsh raindrops. Graham wiped his face to focus on pulling her to safety before she fell off the edge. He took a tentative step forward, but the girl shook her head in response for him not to move. Graham was so close to her.

He reached out. "Take my hand," Graham roared above the thunder.

A mixture of impish delight, seduction, and sorrow lit her face in a smile before she stretched her arms out to the sides and fell backwards off the ledge. Graham screamed and reached out to catch her, but he only caught the emptiness of the air as he plunged to the ground. She had disappeared before him and left him falling.

Falling.

Falling to his impending doom.

Graham Worthington jerked awake, sitting up and gasping for air as the darkness clung to him. His panicked gaze roamed around, and his heart rate slowed as he calmed at the familiar sight of his bedchamber. Collapsing against the pillows, he swiped a hand across his face.

Once he realized he wouldn't fall back to sleep, he rose and drew on his robe. Following the same routine as the other nightmares that haunted his sleep, he moved to the terrace to savor the heady drag of a cigar and a warming shot of whiskey. He sprawled in a chair and tipped his head to stare at the stars. No angry storm taunted him with danger. No. It was a peaceful evening that fooled one into believing goodness was within their reach. However, it was all a sham. Evilness surrounded him, beckoning Graham closer because it wanted to wreak its havoc on him.

It was an evilness Graham swore to obliterate. It had spread its disease long enough. At first he had fought to destroy it because of the injustices it spread while it played its game. But once it struck to torment his family, it became personal. He vowed he would bring about its demise.

Graham threw back two shots of whiskey before lighting his cigar. After taking a long drag, he rested the cigar on the tray provided and rubbed at his temples, but nothing helped to ease the headache that plagued him after his nightmares.

He caused them by the relentless stress he placed on himself to capture Lady Langdale, a notorious mastermind who tormented the wealthy with her vindictive schemes. The investigation had come to a standstill after they captured most of her crew a few weeks ago and locked them behind bars. They had attempted to sabotage the ball his family had thrown to celebrate his two younger sisters' marriages. Lady L had fled and hid underground with the members of her crew that didn't abandon her. She remained elusive, leaving no trace of her whereabouts.

Graham's tortured thoughts caused him another sleepless night. They were a dangerous mix of the unknown, leaving him feeling out of sorts. All because of a lady he had only caught glimpses of. His mystery lady haunted his every thought and vanished whenever he got too close.

He scoured endless musicals, balls, brunches, soirees, all hoping to find her. Since the first evening he saw her at the theater, he had sat through every play and opera, assuming she was a performer. But he never saw her once. She remained a mystery.

But he didn't imagine her. She was as real as the emotions she stirred in him. Fate called them together. Destiny aligned for their souls to meet. She may run away from him all she wanted, but he would catch her eventually. And when he did, she would accept fate's calling just as he had.

Because he didn't dream of the sorrow mixed with determination she held in her gaze before she fell over the edge. He also saw in the depths how she longed for him to catch her. And he would one day.

Another promise he made.

Sabrina understood the risks involved in lurking in the dark shadows as she did now. However, she found more comfort in the darkness than she did under the fresh rays of sunshine. Still, she needed to stay hidden now more than ever. She couldn't risk the exposure or the questioning if someone caught her. Her assignment was far from over. The danger had escalated, making it vital to keep her identity a secret.

However, her craving to live a normal existence led her to spy on the gentleman who held the ability to ruin what she had worked so hard to achieve. If she allowed herself a chance at happiness, it would make her sacrifices worthless. Not to mention, once he learned of her connection to Lady Langdale, he would refuse to acknowledge her.

Every desire she held was nothing but a fanciful imagination never to come true. She needed to keep reminding herself that. Then perhaps she wouldn't face danger every night while she waited outside his terrace, hoping for a glimpse of him. Hoping for him to climb down the trellis and sweep her into his arms. Hoping he would bestow his charming smile on her. Hoping for him to draw her out of the shadows and into the rays of sunshine surrounding him. She must stop wishing for the impossible to occur.

It bothered her to see him so troubled. He should rest comfortably in his bed, not sit in the dark, smoking and drinking. His determination to destroy the evilness of Lady L consumed him. However, Sabrina couldn't allow him to achieve his goal quite yet. She still had much to do.

Sabrina leaned against the tree, fighting back a yawn. She needed to return to safety, but she didn't want to leave him. Not until his troubled mind eased and he returned to bed. Maybe then her guilt would ease a bit for the hardships she caused him and his family.

Sabrina whispered his name. "Graham Worthington. Worth."

His name fit him. Strong, yet playful. While she had yet to enjoy his charming nature, she had studied him enough to understand his character. She watched him mingle with his peers, captivate every lady's attention, and play with his friends' children. He didn't act like an arrogant arse like the other gentlemen she had met this season. But he wasn't too pleasant to keep her from the wanton thoughts, which had led her to him this evening.

Every lady in Graham Worthington's radius wondered how his kisses would feel. Well, wondered about more than kisses, actually. She had heard the whispers of his prowess. Discreet as he may be, it never stopped a lady who enjoyed his magical touch to boast of his attention on them.

Sabrina touched her lips, imagining his mouth pressed against hers. Would he be gentle? Or would he take her lips under his with a force of a passion he barely kept contained? Her fingers trembled at the very thought.

Sabrina turned around. She must leave before she acted on her desires and called out his name. Spying on him had been a mistake, one she must never make again. Because Graham Worthington held the power to destroy her, and a kiss would only be the start of her demise. And she couldn't afford to give herself up to that power.

She had a promise to keep.

Chapter Two

WORTH DRAINED THE TANKARD of ale like a man who enjoyed the disgusting brew, thirsty for more. He slammed it on the table twice to get the barmaid's attention to bring him another. As he waited, he shoveled the slop on the plate into his mouth as if he hadn't eaten for days. At least it held a bit of flavoring and he could stomach it better than the ale. However, it was a far cry from the spread he usually enjoyed for breakfast.

When he first arrived, the tavern owner's wife had waited on him with her brusque manner. A younger, prettier barmaid headed in his direction now, after he had drunk countless mugs of ale and ordered a meal. Worth presumed the girl to be the owner's daughter hoping to earn some extra coin after hearing Worth boast of beating some toffs at cards.

Her father must not care about how Worth wore shabby clothes and looked like a drifter. The tavern owner only cared about what profit he would make from Worth's visit. At least the bloke sent the prettier one his way. He wouldn't mind forgetting his troubles for a spell with a brief flirtation. If it ended with gathering the information he needed, all the better.

"Ah, a right pretty lass to whet me appetite with," Worth slurred with a Scottish accent sure to make his friend Duncan Forrester cringe.

She giggled. "Here is your ale, sir."

Worth smiled at her. So she meant to play the innocent barmaid with him, instead of the sultry one he expected. The girl glanced over her shoulder, looking at her mother, who, Worth noticed, nodded in approval. They thought to play him.

She set the mug down, and Worth slid his hand over hers before she pulled away. He brought her hand to his lips and kissed her knuckles before turning her hand over to slide his tongue across her palm. Instead of her gasping in surprise, interest flashed in her eyes.

She leaned over for him to peruse her ample bosom that was on display. "May I get you anything else?" she asked in a sweet voice.

He pulled her onto his lap. She let out a squeal and slid her arms around his neck in acceptance. "What may you be offering?"

Her annoying giggle echoed in his ear. "Whatever the gentleman desires."

He traced his finger along the valley of her breasts, and her nipples tightened against the thin dress. "I am no gentleman."

The barmaid rubbed her hand against the scruffy beard on his face, scraping her thumb across his bottom lip. "And I am no lady." She squirmed her bottom around on his lap to prove her point.

Worth undid a button on the front of her dress. "Well, that works to my advantage." Another button slipped loose. "Perhaps your father has a bed I may use to *sleep* off my hard night of winning."

She pressed her breasts forward until his hand covered them. "You may use mine."

Worth gave her a wicked grin, squeezing her offerings. "And will you tuck me in, my dear?" He bent to whisper in her ear. "Or better yet, allow me the usage of your soft bosom for a pillow?"

"Only if you make a promise," the barmaid bargained with him.

Worth laughed. "Ah, a greedy wench. But to gain a promise in return, you must supply me with the information I seek."

She pulled back, pouting. "Mama said you would say as much."

"Then your Mama will supply the information for the turn of my coin. I need not make ye any promises." Worth pretended to rise.

"No. No." She pressed a hand on his chest, and he settled back on the bench. "Mama will never tell you the information you seek."

Worth narrowed his gaze. "So ye both thought to play me false?"

The barmaid glanced nervously over her shoulder and confessed once she noticed her mother was busy. "I was to lure you to my bed with promises of giving you information. Once we reached my room, I was to give you a drink laced with a sleeping potion to make you pass out."

"Then let me guess, you would steal my coin and pretend your innocence. Then your father would throw me out of the tavern after a beating because I stole his daughter's virtue. Am I correct?" Worth arched an eyebrow.

The barmaid nodded, appearing anything but ashamed of what they had planned for him. She wore a devious smile as she slid her hand down his chest and to his lap. "I believe we can all get our way."

Worth grabbed her wrist. "I do not see how I win. What, with lost moments of my time and an empty purse."

"I am willing to negotiate, my lord."

He jerked on her wrist to make his point clear. "I already told you I am no gentleman."

"Nor am I a proper miss."

"Then what is your proposition?" Worth growled.

"Follow me upstairs, where we can come to amicable terms without my parents hearing the details."

"Do you take me for a fool? I no sooner step abovestairs and meet the demise you laid out for me," Worth accused.

"To show my intentions are pure, I will answer one question. If you wish to learn more, you must follow. Remember, a promise for a promise."

Worth studied the barmaid for any signs that she meant to double-cross him, but he saw none. If he thought he had her figured right, she only sought to satisfy her urges without her parents' knowledge. He wanted no part of her plans in that regard, but she didn't need to learn that until he gained his information.

"I am searching for a lady who hides in your midst. She yields much power. I need to know where to find her," Worth said.

The barmaid narrowed her gaze. "Are you friend or foe?"

Worth caressed her arm. "Is that any concern of yours?"

The barmaid's eyelids grew heavy at his attention. "She hides in a house nearby."

"Where?" He gripped her harder at this news.

Her features tightened from his brutal treatment, but it didn't stop her from making bold suggestions. "Follow me and you shall seek your information."

She slid off his lap and held out her hand. Worth hesitated for only a brief second before swearing under his breath. After throwing the coins to cover his meal and drinks on the table slab, he wrapped his arm around the barmaid's waist and nuzzled her neck. He needed to fool her parents that she had charmed him to leave. She played along, much to his relief.

He followed her through the tavern to a set of stairs nestled near the rear of the building. Someone shoved him from behind, knocking him to his knees before he climbed the stairs. With a swiftness he never expected, a young lad swiped the purse from his pocket and tore out the back door.

Worth jumped to his feet, slapping away the hands of the barmaid in her attempt to help him. He didn't know if this was part of their scam. Or if the boy had noticed his coin and decided he was an easy mark to pickpocket. He tore after the lad, knocking people out of his way and jumping over crates in his attempt to snag the boy. But the lad was swift on his feet and lost himself in the crowd.

When Worth saw the boy sneaking down an alley, he followed, confident he had trapped the pickpocket. But when he rounded the corner, the alleyway split off into two different paths. He ran to the center point and turned around in a circle. He had lost the boy.

"Damn," Worth growled.

Not only had he lost his bag of coins, but he also lost his chance to gain the information he desperately needed. It was impossible for him to return to the tavern and strike the same deal. It would risk the livelihood of the family who owned the tavern. Even though they meant to scam him, he wouldn't risk their lives.

He had seen the damage Lady L delivered to those who betrayed her. She was even more dangerous since her plans had fallen apart. However, she still held the advantage by keeping herself hidden with a cleverness they had yet to figure out. The most maddening part was how she hid in plain sight, yet they were blind to her whereabouts. He'd stood on the verge of having his blinders lifted, and the measly street urchin had stolen it from him.

The thief held no connection with the tavern owner but stole from him of his own free will. What made it worse for his ego was how it wasn't a boy who swiped his money but a mere girl. A girl who bobbed and weaved through the obstacles as if she danced across a ballroom floor. Her movements were fluid and graceful with the elegance of a fine lady, not a street urchin. The trousers molded to her form like a tight glove, and when she turned her head over her shoulder to judge how close he was, he noticed the softness of her face. Her high cheekbones, pouty lips, and the arch of her eyebrows as she glared at him. But most of all, he admired the determination in her gaze to escape him.

She had won, and yet he chuckled at how she had bested him. Oh, his family would show no mercy in their teasing if they saw him now. Especially since the girl reminded him of his younger sister, Maggie, who had dressed like a lad for most of her life. Until recently, since her marriage to Crispin Dracott. Maggie never held the skill to outrun him and he always caught her when she tried to escape his capture from her hijinks.

However, this girl had escaped and left Worth wondering about her identity. Perhaps he only wondered because she reminded him of someone. With the nightmares that disrupted his sleep and his constant search for Lady Langdale, everyone's faces started blending together. Hell, he hadn't even eaten a meal with his family for weeks. Perhaps he should take a day to reflect and relax with his family, then start with a fresh outlook. If not, he would surely go mad. Then he would be worthless to the case.

After all, it wasn't as if Lady Langdale planned to go anywhere.

Chapter Three

S ABRINA GLANCED OVER HER shoulder and saw she was within his grasp. She spun around to avoid running into a group of sailors, slipped down the alleyway, and ran to where the path split off into two different directions. If she fled along either path, he would spot her and continue chasing her. Sabrina slipped behind a stack of crates, catching her breath.

Soon Graham Worthington sprinted down the alley and came to a halt. He turned slowly, pondering which direction to go. She hid because she assumed he would choose a path to chase her down. Sabrina held her breath, hoping he wouldn't find her when she remained close. The sound of her erratic breathing was deafening in her ears, and she wondered if he heard her. Then her panic subsided once she realized she imagined the volume of her breathing.

When he remained in the alley without searching for her, Sabrina grew confused. He acted peculiar, considering his bag of coins had been stolen, and he had lost his chance to gain Lady L's whereabouts. After swearing his frustration, he chuckled as if he found the thrill of chasing her amusing.

Sabrina slid along the building, clutching the coin purse in her lap as she watched him. The smile on his face grew, and he whistled a merry tune as he strolled back to the storefronts.

She didn't dare peek her head around the crates for one last look at him, even though she desperately wanted to.

She waited for an hour before she ventured out of her hiding spot. However, she should have waited a while longer.

Crispin Dracott leaned against the opposite building. Once she emerged, he held out his hand. She stalked over to him and dropped the bag of coins onto his palm. Then she turned and started along a path. Sabrina was mistaken to believe handing over the money was the end of their meeting. When Dracott caught up with her and walked along silently, she knew it was only a matter of time before she must endure his lecture.

However, he never spoke a word. Instead, he walked along with her as he used to when they had attempted these ploys in the past. They used to work as a team, until Dracott had abandoned her for his brother. Not that stealing Worth's coins was a ploy. She had done so to stop the barmaid from giving him information about Lady Langdale. Sabrina needed to protect the lady a while longer until she gained what she needed. If Worth learned of Lady L, then he would discover her too. Her heart might cry out with longing for that chance, but she was realistic enough to understand the disastrous repercussion that would occur.

Sabrina broke the silence first. "I am not leading you to her."

Dracott kept his stride alongside hers. "I know. Perhaps I wish to take a walk with my friend."

"Friend?" Sabrina scoffed. "Aren't ye a bit too high and mighty for the likes of me?"

Dracott stopped walking and grabbed her arm to stop her. When she stared at his grip, he dropped his hand. "Why do you insist on keeping with this charade? Allow us to help you."

Sabrina stepped forward, glaring at him. "I should not have to explain myself to you. You know why I continue to stay."

She shook her head. "How can you possibly help me? She has proven how devious and manipulative she is. No. I am better off sticking with my agenda."

Dracott stuffed his hands into his pockets. "Why did you mark him today?"

"Because he is damn vulnerable out in the open like he is. Not to mention naïve about how the underbelly of London works. He was a sitting target, and I needed to teach him a lesson." Sabrina shook her head at Worth's actions. "If not, then he would've met a more unfortunate accident if he climbed those steps."

"I am sure Worth could've taken care of himself."

Sabrina harrumphed. "Not against three of Lady L's guards who sat waiting for him."

Dracott raked his hands through his hair. "Damn! We hadn't seen them."

Sabrina smirked. "You can thank me later. For now, we must part ways, *my friend*."

"Ren, please reconsider," Dracott pleaded.

Ren swept her hat off and bowed. "Until another day, my lord."

Dracott scowled at her sarcasm and threw out his own taunt after she took a few steps. "Oh, and be careful on your next visit to gaze upon him throughout the night. The guards noticed your footprints near the tree. I pondered what your motive might be. However, after you protected him today, I realize you care for him." Dracott paused. "While a dangerous emotion to have during this unstable time, it can offer you the happiness you deserve."

Sabrina stopped walking when Dracott mentioned how careless she was in destroying the evidence of her obsession. His next words bothered her with how close he was to the truth of her infatuation with his brother-in-law. However, when she turned to deny his accusations, she stood alone. Dracott had disappeared as easily as he appeared. What bothered Sabrina was how oblivious she was to Dracott while she watched over Worth.

Her only focus was keeping him safe. This morning, Sabrina had overheard Lady L sending her guards to the tavern after learning Worth snooped around. Sabrina had snuck out and followed after the guards, then she set up a position inside the tavern, sitting behind two sailors. She had blended into the woodwork and waited for Worth to ask questions.

However, she had been unprepared to see him shamelessly flirt with the barmaid. He appeared to fall for the innocent act she played. When he pulled the wench onto his lap, her stomach had dropped and an unknown emotion coursed through her. When the barmaid wrapped her hand against his cheek, Sabrina had wanted to leap to her feet and rip the girl off his lap, then scratch the wench's face for even soiling him with her touch.

Each second had crawled by, and her irritation had clawed at her to make a scene. Instead, she had waited to make her move. When the wench had held out her hand for Worth to follow her and he accepted it by wrapping his arm around her waist, Sabrina knew she must cause a distraction to lure him away. She had thought of the perfect scene to cause after she remembered Worth had flashed his coin, bragging about beating some toffs at cards.

Sabrina stole the purse of coins and ran away. If she was honest, she would admit how exhilarating the chase was. She came alive with each twist and turn she eluded him with. A thrill coursed through her veins that she wished to experience more of. It carried the same euphoria of each occasion when he almost held her within his grasp.

Only he was clueless about her multiple identities.

Dracott dropped a bag of coins in front of him on his desk. Worth had returned to the office to inform Ralston how he planned to rest for a few days before resuming his search. After they discussed their next step, Ralston had left, and he had waited for Dracott's return. They had agreed to meet there after their venture this morning ended. However, he never expected the return of his bag of coins.

He looked up at Dracott. "Ye didn't have to wrestle the wee lass for the bit of coin, did ye, mate?"

Dracott shook his head. "Please stop with your awful accent. It was probably what gave you away."

Worth leaned back in his chair and folded his hands atop his stomach. "Aye. And because I've gotten sloppy. I am preoccupied and plagued with sleepless nights."

Dracott sat down across from him. "What troubles you?"

Worth scoffed. "Really?"

Dracott frowned. "Besides the obvious. Lady Langdale's underground hiding has become a common occurrence that is normal for the investigation. You should hold relief at how we've hindered her efforts since capturing more than half of her organization. She works with a skeletal crew that can do no harm. Unless you continue to proceed without caution."

Worth nodded. "I plan to enjoy a rest before I refocus the search again."

Dracott sat forward. "An excellent idea. In the meantime, I will see what I can uncover. You were close today. I could feel it."

Worth shook his head. "No. The results of today happened because we both need a break. You need time alone with Maggie since you've yet to enjoy a honeymoon. I talked with

Ralston and we've decided to lie low, hoping it might make Lady L feel comfortable to make her connections again."

"Clever and it might work," Dracott said.

"I hope so. Now, back to how you recovered my coin from the lass."

Dracott cleared his throat. "Why do you assume it was a girl? I thought it was a lad."

Worth barked out a laugh. "You, of all people, should have noticed the girl wore a disguise."

Dracott smiled. "What can I say? I only have eyes for Maggie. Either way, when you walked out of the alley, I figured the thief found a hiding spot."

Worth frowned. "I thought she ran along a path."

"She banked on that. It is an old ploy, one where you confuse the con. They are unsure which path to take, while you hide in plain sight. I waited for the thief, tripped him, and took back your bag of coin. The lad was too frightened, and he fled away," Dracott explained.

"She," Worth emphasized.

"Right, she. Anyway, you lost your chance to learn more but not your coin."

"Did you recognize anything familiar about her?" Worth asked.

Dracott stilled. He hated betraying Worth. The gentleman had accepted his past without judgement and they were now family. However, Ren had been his family for more years than he could count. It didn't matter that they didn't share the same blood. He considered Sabrina his family, too. Only he couldn't admit to knowing her until she decided so. For now, he would keep her secret, but the day for her to reveal herself was upon them. He only hoped it wasn't too late for her. However, he feared it might be.

"No. She seemed like your usual street urchin stealing the coin of an innocent man," Dracott lied. "Why? Did she appear familiar to you?"

Worth stood up. "I must be mistaken. 'Tis all. Shall we join the ladies for luncheon?"

Dracott followed Worth outside to the carriage. Before he entered, he saw that Sabrina had chosen not to follow his advice because she stood across the street, taunting him. Worth wasn't the only foolish one who acted sloppily. He sent her a signal that he noticed her, but she refused to acknowledge it. Instead, she stepped out in front of the crowd, flaunting how his warnings meant nothing to her. There was no more he could do. He climbed inside and kept Worth distracted by telling him of Maggie's latest hijinks. He breathed a sigh of relief when Worth didn't see Ren across the street. Because if he had, Dracott held no clue how he would react.

And for that, Sabrina should thank her lucky stars. Because then she would never achieve the success of her plan she so desperately craved.

Chapter Four

"LOOK WHO HAS DECIDED to grace us with his presence today." Eden patted her brother's cheek before sitting down next to him at the dining table. "Bristly face and all."

"Yes, it is nice to have my family all together once again." Lady Worthington frowned. "Even if they insist on dining with us in their unkept manner."

Graham unfolded the napkin on his lap. "I apologize for my appearance, Mother. But it is necessary for my work."

"We will discuss none of that nonsense at the dining table," Lady Worthington reprimanded him.

"The beard makes Graham quite dashing," Evelyn complimented.

Graham winked at his sister-in-law. "I knew your taste leaned toward an adventurous gentleman than the sour earl you married."

"I've warned you before, and I will not do so again. Focus your flirtation elsewhere," Reese growled in warning.

"Oh, Reese is the least sour gentleman I know." Evelyn gazed adoringly at her husband while everyone else groaned. "And, my dear, please allow your brother to practice his flirtation." Her tone dropped to a dramatic whisper. "I fear his charming nature is a bit out of practice. Plus, it boosts my ego as huge as I've grown."

"You are not huge one bit but as beautiful as the day I stole our first kiss." Reese placed his hand lovingly over Evelyn's increased stomach.

Evelyn covered his hand as the baby kicked against their palms. "And you are as sweet today as you were then."

Graham coughed. "Reese, sweet? Need I remind you, dear Evelyn, of how he thought you were your sister Charlie?"

Evelyn gazed into Reese's eyes. "But his heart knew the truth."

"Aye, it did, my love."

Graham shook his head, laughing. "I love how you've turned into such a sap."

"Graham Edward Worthington, do not mock the love Reese and Evelyn share," Lady Worthington reprimanded him. "Your time will soon come and then you'll understand what you've missed all these years."

Graham cut the food on his plate. "I apologize." He directed his knife around the table, pointing at his siblings and their spouses. "However, I refuse to fall into the same trap as the rest of you."

Eden laughed beside him. "He declares that as if he has a choice."

Graham arched his eyebrow at her. "I do."

Eden patted his cheek again. "Sure you do."

"Do you not have your own home to eat luncheon at?" Graham growled.

"Mama invited us." Eden smirked. "She wanted to hear of our plans for when the baby comes."

Graham glanced between Evelyn and Eden. "Why would you have any plans when their next pipsqueak is born?"

Eden leaned over to whisper. "Because 'tis not their pipsqueak we are discussing but my own."

Graham sat back in shock. "Serious?"

Eden nodded.

Graham looked around the table to gauge everyone else's reactions, but they appeared as if they already knew. He turned back to Eden. "Am I the last to learn of this wonderful news?"

Eden clutched his hands. "We shared it last week at dinner and have arrived for every meal this week, waiting for you to arrive to share with you. But you've been a ghost, flittering in and out."

Graham stood and wrapped Eden in a hug, twirling her around. "I am so happy for you, sis." He stretched out his hand to Falcone. "Congratulations, my friend."

Falcone shook Graham's hand. "My wife is officially out of commission."

"Agreed. And so are you," Graham informed Falcone.

Falcone smirked. "No, I am not. My shoulder has healed, and I will return soon."

Graham helped Eden back into her chair. "No. I'll not allow you in harm's path with a babe on the way."

"I think I speak for myself, Ravencroft, and Dracott when I say we will not step aside until we capture Lady Langdale and watch her hang for her offenses," Falcone stated.

"Agreed," Ravencroft seconded.

"I agree too," Dracott said.

Graham pinched his lips, staring at the determination on their faces, and realized no matter how much he protested, everyone at the table would overrule his decision. They were a family who stood by each other through thick and thin. He looked at his mother, hoping she would help make his point clear. However, she only smiled at him. They outnumbered him.

"Fine," Graham growled.

It didn't take for the silence to change to their usual animated discussions. He sat watching his siblings in their happiness and felt nothing but pure joy at how they had found their soul mates. Before long, his mother would make her attempts to see him settled with a bride of his own. What was it about mothers having to marry off their offspring? Graham had thought his mother would've been different on that accord, considering how her marriage had ended. But then again, all his mother had ever strived for was their happiness.

His gaze landed on Maggie, and his mouth tugged into a grin. Maggie made the most surprising change of them all. He never expected her to marry during her first season, especially when she had begged him to help her convince their mother that she wasn't ready. Not only had she gotten married, but she had also traded her breeches in for the flowing dresses his mother used to have to fight her to wear.

Maggie snapped her fingers to get his attention. "Why are you staring at me so strangely?"

"You remind me of someone I chased after today." Graham smiled as he remembered the graceful way the girl avoided him.

Maggie's face scrunched up in confusion. "Why were you chasing after a girl?"

Dracott scoffed. "Because your brother thought he chased after a young boy who stole his bag of coins."

"But it was a girl?" Maggie's eyes lit up at the possibility.

Dracott nodded. "Aye."

"Did he catch her?" Maggie asked.

Dracott laughed. "No, she outran him and got away."

Maggie clapped her hands. "Oh, that is so hilarious."

"Graham must have slowed down with his advanced age. Perhaps we should get him settled soon, Mama, or else he will not have the energy for a new bride," Noel teased.

Graham glared at his other sister. "And what is your reason for eating here this afternoon, brat?"

Noel beamed. "Because Evelyn promised to help me with my costume for the ball we are attending this evening."

"Which ball shall that be?" Graham asked.

Noel bounced in her chair. "The Cadburys are holding a costume ball this evening. Will you come?"

Graham stood up, dropping the napkin on the plate. "I wouldn't miss it for the world."

Noel let out a squeal. "Yes, we will have so much fun this evening."

Graham chuckled and walked over to kiss his mother's cheek. "Thank you for the enlightening luncheon."

"You're welcome, my dear. It was nice to see you, if only for a short while. Will you at least do me a favor?"

"It depends," Graham teased.

"Please take a razor to your cheeks," Lady Worthington requested.

"I promise after the ball. After all, a pirate cannot walk amongst the ton with a shaven face. How else will they fear me?" Graham laughed on his way out of the dining room.

"We need to get that boy settled before he continues to wreak havoc on his life," Lady Worthington muttered.

Eden glanced at Evelyn, smiling. "Evelyn has found the perfect lady for him."

"Mmm," Lady Worthington murmured. "Will she also be in attendance this evening?"

Evelyn nodded. "I believe so."

Lady Worthington lifted her teacup. "Then to the fall of your brother. May he fall the hardest of you all."

The table laughed at Lady Worthington's toast. Not one person held an ounce of pity for Graham. They were out to conspire against him.

Hopefully, love prevailed for Graham.

Chapter Five

G RAHAM LEANED AGAINST THE pillar, watching the guests in various stages of costumes. The guests wore the standard storybook character, various people of history, and the ones with no imagination wore a mask. His favorite to admire were the ladies who wore scandalous costumes, more daring than their normal dress. Those were the ones he admired throughout the evening. Because the ladies grew bolder in their scant attire, propositioning him after several glasses of champagne. The ladies would approach him and whisper their desire for him to plunder their bodies, if he so wished. A tempting offer he kept refusing, much to their disappointed pouts.

He tipped the flute to his mouth and let the champagne cool his throat. His gaze swept through the crowd again. Perhaps he should accept one of those offers after all. It wasn't as if his mystery lady would appear to lift him from his misery. Graham pushed himself off the pillar to weave through the crowd in his search for amusement. He nodded to a group of friends but didn't stop to speak with them. His quest to find a lover for the evening became his new plan to ease away his stress.

Graham came to a stop when he noticed his sisters and sister-in-law surrounding a lady. When Noel spotted him, she waved him over. He turned around and started off in the opposite direction. He refused to allow them to trap him into dancing or spending time with someone of their choosing. No. This evening was about his own personal gratification.

However, he walked into a trap. Walking in his direction were two of his new brothers-in-law, Dracott and Ravencroft. He glanced over his shoulder and saw Maggie break off from the circle to pursue him. He only hoped to gain their sympathy and rely on their male camaraderie.

Graham stopped before them, reaching out to slap them both on the arm. "Do a bloke a favor and charm your wives' attention off of me for the evening?"

Dracott winced. "Sorry. Maggie has already waved us down to stall you."

"Whipped," Graham muttered under his breath.

Ravencroft smirked. "Ahh, but 'tis most pleasurable."

Graham grimaced. "Please, have mercy. I do not wish to listen to your bedroom activities."

Ravencroft shrugged. "Only pointing out the benefits of marriage."

Dracott looked at Ravencroft. "I think it was more along the lines of how he didn't wish to picture his sister in relation to the topic."

Ravencroft nodded. "Yes. I can understand how a brother would find the topic uncomfortable in relation to his sister."

Graham gritted his teeth over their amusement at his expense. "Will you two please move?"

Before they moved, Maggie was upon him. Her hand clutched at his arm, tugging until he turned to face her. "Come with me, Graham. You must meet Evelyn's new friend. She is amazing and not to mention pretty."

"Pretty?" Graham winced. He understood what pretty entailed. It was a polite term ladies used to describe another lady who was as plain as dirt. He didn't consider himself a shallow gentleman. However, he preferred a lady who held an exotic beauty. Because the pretty ones didn't hold the ability to carry a conversation and were meek and obedient. He loved a lady who carried passion in her soul like a second skin. Who challenged him with her wit and other pleasurable traits.

"Well, not exactly pretty." Maggie paused, twisting her lips from side to side in her attempt to make the lady more appealing. "She is more . . . ahh, I don't know how to describe her. Just come and meet her. You will see for yourself."

Graham attempted to gain Maggie's support. "I thought I could count on you to take my side."

"The same way you assisted me after I begged for your help? I will offer you the same advice you gave me. 'One cannot fight the inevitable. It is a pastime. You must embrace it.'"

Graham scoffed. "Those were not my words."

Maggie smirked. "Close enough."

Graham peered over his shoulder, hoping Dracott and Ravencroft would hold any pity for him, but they shook their head at him. Short of causing a scene over not wanting an introduction to this *pretty* lady, Graham held no other options. He allowed Maggie to drag him along. Best to get it over with. He would offer a dance and return the girl to her chaperone. Then he would resume his pursuit of finding a bed partner for the remainder of the evening.

Sabrina stood in a state of panic. The ladies she talked with turned their back on her to witness their brother coming over to them. She pressed her hand to her face to make sure the mask remained in place so they couldn't witness the terror crossing her features. She was a fool to push her luck. At first, she had shared a simple conversation with her new friend, then more ladies had joined in. Sabrina thought she had blown her cover when Dracott's and Ravencroft's wives gushed over her costume. However, neither of them recognized her. Still, she pushed the boundaries by remaining in the small circle.

Her first mistake was the friendship she struck with Evelyn Worthington. She had never realized who the countess was when they first met. They had each stolen away for a spell during a ball and started a conversation. They had shared a discussion where she didn't have to pretend to be anyone but herself. They had discussed their love of books. Evelyn had shared her favorite bookstores in London after Sabrina mentioned how she had spent the past few years living abroad. Her new friend never asked any intrusive questions, only offered Sabrina a glimpse of a simple life. Throughout their entire visit, they had never once exchanged names. Sabrina had left their visit feeling relieved because she didn't want to lie to the kind lady or risk Evelyn's life for showing Sabrina a moment of kindness.

It wasn't until they bumped into each other this evening that Sabrina learned her new friend was none other than Evelyn Worthington. The repercussions of not learning the identity of Reese Worthington's wife would be insurmountable if Lady L ever learned of her mistake. In her obsession with Graham Worthington, Sabrina had neglected to learn the key players of Lady L's revenge. Especially when Evelyn was the prime target. Lady L's bitterness over Reese Worthington throwing her over for the lovely debutante still rankled the lady. It was because of their marriage and Evelyn's connection to Colebourne, who had exiled Lady Langdale, that made her the target for the villainess's revenge.

Evelyn had caught Sabrina by surprise when she recognized her in the costume she wore. She wore a mask of sequins and had painted her wig in a variety of colors to disguise her hair. Evelyn had raved about how original Sabrina's costume was and how she must let her introduce her to her brother-in-law. Since she hadn't known Evelyn's identity yet, she had smiled her agreement on the introduction and wondered if meeting another gentleman would pull her out of her musings and help her focus on her mission. Not to mention how she longed for any sort of companionship. A sense of loneliness had clung to her since Dracott abandoned her.

While Evelyn exclaimed over the brilliance of Sabrina's costume, her sister-in-law had joined them. That was the start of Sabrina's panic. She had recognized the beautiful Eden Worthington, now Eden Falcone. Sabrina had made sure their paths never crossed because she knew how the lady worked for her brother to gather information. Eden never gave any indication that she held a clue who Sabrina was.

Eden's eyes were lit with curiosity as her gaze fell upon Sabrina. "Evelyn, is this the wonderful creature you were describing for Graham?"

Sabrina tried not to choke on the champagne she drank to calm her nerves. Evelyn? Graham? Oh, what had she done? She had made herself a target with her longing for a simple friendship not clouded in deceit. However, as much as she panicked, her heart gave a slight flutter at how they thought her worthy enough for Graham.

"Yes. Eden, this is . . ." Evelyn gasped. "Oh, how terribly rude of me. We never exchanged names and here I am plotting for you to meet my brother-in-law." Then Evelyn did something unexpected. She wrapped her hands around Sabrina's hand. "I am Evelyn Worthington, and this is my sister-in-law, Eden Falcone."

"Sabrina," she blurted out when they stared at her.

"Sabrina?" Eden asked, waiting to hear her surname.

"Sabrina Lan—" Sabrina paused, because she couldn't very well tell them her last name. She cleared her throat. "Sabrina Lancaster." It wasn't a complete lie. Lancaster was her mother's maiden name.

Eden smiled at her acceptance. "Nice to meet you, Sabrina. Evelyn has told us so much about you already."

"She has?" Sabrina looked at Evelyn in confusion.

Evelyn blushed. "I hope I wasn't too presumptuous. We shared a friendly connection when we chatted and I had hoped a friendship would blossom from it."

Sabrina allowed herself to relax after Evelyn's genuine confession, and the three of them fell into a friendly conversation. That was, until Eden's two sisters joined their small circle. Sabrina grew tense, waiting for them to expose her true identity. However, her costume must have distracted them from recognizing her. As she stood listening to their friendly banter, Sabrina understood how Dracott and Ravencroft had fallen in love with Maggie and Noel. The two ladies held such admirable qualities she had never expected. However, she still suffered the bitter sting of Dracott's betrayal.

"Look, there is Graham now. What perfect timing. The next waltz is about to begin," Noel gushed.

Maggie grabbed Sabrina's hand and squeezed it, catching Sabrina unprepared again for their affectionate attentions. "Oh, you two will hit it off."

If Sabrina didn't leave soon, she feared a panic attack would consume her. She played with fire by conversing with these ladies for this long. She couldn't afford to risk meeting Graham Worthington.

However, her luck continued when Graham turned in the opposite direction, away from them. Now, she must excuse herself to return to her chaperone. An imaginary character on her part, but the excuse would pacify the other ladies.

Eden chuckled. "Coward."

"Mama said it would not be an easy feat to accomplish," Noel added.

"I will get him," Maggie said before taking off.

The other ladies turned to watch Maggie's exchange with Graham. They all stood in front of her, blocking him from seeing her. As much as their actions were to her advantage, a part of her wished his gaze held a spark of interest.

Sabrina peeked over Evelyn's shoulder and watched Maggie convince her brother to meet her. However, following behind them were Dracott and Ravencroft. Her costume would never fool them. They would recognize her immediately. And while Dracott might keep her identity a secret, Ravencroft wouldn't. He had never trusted her motives, especially when it involved Dracott, and he would find pleasure in exposing her to her new friends.

She didn't need another sign to show her how she needed to sneak away. It was a necessity for her survival. Sabrina took a few steps backwards. Once she noticed how they didn't see her escape, she turned to blend in with a fresh wave of guests walking past their group. She never stopped until she reached the gardens. Sabrina collapsed on a bench, clutching her racing heart. She had avoided a catastrophe. Tonight's incident was a warning for her to refocus on her goals. If not, then every sacrifice she had made held no meaning. And all for what? An illusion.

One she must stop indulging in.

When Graham joined his family, his sisters smirked their enjoyment at besting him, and Evelyn gave him a devious smile, one his sister-in-law never wore, but it gave him proof of how they attempted to help his mother find him a bride. Starting with Evelyn's *pretty* new friend. Graham fought back the shudders and pasted on a charming smile. One he hoped fooled his family and showed the girl he wasn't a total louse after he danced with her and discarded her as he planned.

"So, who is this paragon of virtue I *must* meet?" Graham asked.

Evelyn hooked her arm through Graham's. "Allow us to introduce you to the lovely Sabrina."

"Lovely too? Maggie only mentioned she was pretty," Graham quipped.

"Oh, that too." Evelyn motioned for his sisters to separate.

Noel and Eden stepped away and watched Graham for his reaction. When he held a blank expression at the empty spot behind them, they turned and noticed their friend had played a disappearing act. Graham didn't know whether to feel offended or relieved the lady didn't wish to meet him, either. She was probably too insecure and fled while his sisters found amusement in trapping him. Graham laughed at how swiftly the amusement turned on them.

"Yes. She is quite *pretty*. Pretty imaginable." Graham laughed. "Perhaps next time you will have better luck when trying to lay your trap."

Evelyn stood on her tiptoes, searching the crowd for any sign of Sabrina. But she was too short to see above so many tall shoulders. She looked at Eden in question, but Eden only shrugged. Neither of them knew Sabrina well enough to understand why she would've fled.

"Did you say Sabrina?" Ravencroft asked.

Noel moved to her husband's side. "Yes. Sabrina Lancaster. Have you met her before?"

Graham noticed the swift look Ravencroft and Dracott shared before Ravencroft smiled at Noel to cover his curiosity. "No, never heard of her."

The answer seemed to pacify his sister, and Graham was about to question him further, but a young girl moving swiftly out the terrace doors caught his attention. Her costume was a magnificent creation in the way it hugged her curves. While she hurried, she still carried herself with grace. A memory tugged at his conscience, but he ignored it in his need to catch up to her before she slipped away.

He had found his conquest for the evening and no longer needed to amuse his family.

"Excuse me," he mumbled before leaving them.

Before he left, he overheard Maggie exclaim to Dracott, "You should have seen her costume. She was a mer . . ." The rest of Maggie's description got lost as he moved farther away. But he didn't care, anyway. The lady was an obligation he was thankful he didn't have to accommodate his family with.

He stepped onto the terrace, searching the grounds for the lady. The glittering sequins of her costume reflected against the moonlight, guiding Graham in her direction. She flittered through the maze as if she had memorized it. When he reached her, he found her on a bench, clutching her heart.

"I hope you are only clutching your heart because you are relieved to have escaped your family from setting you up with a stranger and not because you are ill," Graham spoke softly at her, so he didn't frighten her away.

Sabrina gasped and jumped to her feet. She thought she was alone and no one had followed her. Instead, the gentleman who starred in her every fantasy stood a few feet away from her.

"Is that the reason for your escape to the gardens?" Sabrina flirted back.

Obviously, she had never learned her lesson from befriending the gentleman's family. But she couldn't resist the opportunity to share a moment alone with him. To have his complete attention focused only on her.

Graham bit back the groan he wanted to exhale as he took in the full effect of her costume. The sequined gown clung to every curve on her body, displaying her ripe breasts for his viewing pleasure. Her hair was an exotic mixture of every color of the rainbow, streaming along her back. She had secured the glorious strands with sequined hair clips. A mask decorated with the same colors hid her face from view. Even though she kept herself hidden, he knew she was a beauty unlike any had ever seen before.

The bodice of her gown fit snugly against her breasts, while the skirt wrapped around her form in a spiral of a mermaid's tail. How he had missed spotting her in the ballroom amazed him. Also, how no other gentlemen whispered of the exquisite creature was beyond him. The dress was in no way demure; no, it was meant to entice every gentleman to answer her siren call.

He stepped closer, entranced by how she flirted with him in return. The husky softness of her voice called to him. "Yes, it was urgent I flee while I still held a chance."

Sabrina moved toward the fountain, putting much-needed distance between them. While she wasn't ready to make another escape, she didn't dare let him any closer. She feared her resistance would crumble. "Why?"

Graham shuddered. "Because my sister described the girl as *pretty*."

Sabrina giggled, trailing her fingers in the water. "And is pretty such a terrible trait for a girl to hold?"

Graham sighed. "The worst."

"Oh." Sabrina didn't know any other way to respond. For Maggie to say she was pretty, she took that as the highest compliment, considering how beautiful Maggie, her sisters, and Evelyn were. Sabrina paled compared to them.

Damn. What did he say to offend her? "Unlike you." What in the hell did he mean by that comment? She had him so flustered that he lost his ability to charm her. He tried to smile, but she only frowned at him.

"How so?"

Her simple question gave him all the hope he needed to turn this conversation to his advantage. "First of all, your costume entices every male around to follow in your wake."

"What if I only wish to entice one certain gentleman to follow me?" Sabrina held no clue what gave her the nerve to speak so boldly.

Graham didn't answer her question but continued with how amazing he thought she looked. "Your features tease of an amazing beauty I wish to see more of. May I remove your mask?"

Sabrina walked around the fountain, reaching up to make sure her mask stayed in place. "Perhaps we should keep the aura of mystery surrounding us, my pirate lord. Also, I would not wish to disappoint you with my *pretty* features."

For every step she tried to keep between them, he moved forward. "Oh, you will not change my mind on the opinion I hold of the beauty you keep hidden. Will you at least tell me your name?"

Sabrina shook her head.

Graham stopped but a breath away from her. "Then I shall call you Siren."

Sabrina held her breath at his closeness. Her hand itched to caress his rough cheek. To feel the bristles tickle her fingertips.

Graham stood still. She didn't realize she had lifted her hand to stroke her fingers against his rough cheek. Especially when her eyes displayed the intense desire she held her body back from. He slowly lifted his hand and pressed it against hers, holding it to his cheek while his mouth brushed across hers. A soft sigh whispered past her lips and into his soul.

He was powerless to resist her any longer. Graham wrapped his arm around her waist, pulled her close, and kissed her. A kiss so soft he thought he imagined it. But when her lips parted and their kiss deepened, his heart declared the caress wasn't a figment of his imagination, but an act so real it awakened all his senses. He dipped his tongue inside to dance alongside hers. Graham savored the sweetness of the champagne as he devoured her.

Sabrina refused to listen to the warning bells ringing all around her. How could this emotionally charged act be anything but what fate demanded? Two souls lost in the passion that destiny had set forth for them. It never registered with her how she had touched him until he held her hand pressed to his cheek. She thought her imagination stretched to experience the tingling sensation she felt from his warmth searing into her fingertips.

His gentle kiss showed Sabrina the rumors of his character were true. She listened to the whispers of how generous a lover he was, one who always gifted a lady with his special attention. She might be naïve to the other sex, but Graham Worthington held the experience to seduce her senseless. Also, the skill with which he stole a kiss from her lips showed his ability to please a woman.

Sabrina moaned when Graham increased the pressure of the kiss. It changed from gentle persuasion to demanding need. She lost herself in the twisting onslaught of passion binding them together and poured her own desperation into the act. The bristles on his face scraped her hand as she sank her fingers into the thick mane of his hair, dislodging the que that held his locks from his face.

Graham drank the passion from the siren's lips. It poured over with each nip of his lips against hers. Her moans echoed around them. He hungered to kiss every inch of her over and over all throughout the night and listen to the sweet melody of her call.

He pulled back, gasping for breath. Once he saw the need pleading for him to never stop in her gaze, Graham dipped his head again and continued kissing her. Everything about her drew on his addiction to claim her for himself. It didn't matter that he knew nothing of her, even her name. His soul spoke to him about how she was the one and it was the only sign he needed.

"My sweet mermaid, can I tempt you back to the sea on my ship?" Graham whispered his request.

Sabrina couldn't help but smile at his attempt to jest over their costumes. "The other mermaids whisper of how your offer is an attempt to lure me on a voyage so I might reveal where the hidden treasure is located."

"If the hidden treasure holds the key to your heart, then you leave me with no choice but to kidnap and tie you to my bed until you confess your secret." Graham found her amusing. Most ladies would roll their eyes at his humor, but she played along.

When she pulled out of his arms, the loss gave him pause. He feared she would refuse his offer.

Sabrina smiled wistfully. "Ah, but I would not last long. Even now I am on the verge of perishing without my beloved water flowing around me."

Graham grabbed her hand, toying with her fingers. "Yet you still give me hope, my tempting siren."

"How is that, my pirate lord?" Oh my, he was so handsome with his confident smile and the eyepatch covering one of his eyes.

"You never denied the treasure held the key to your heart."

"Because there is no treasure, only the lure of my siren's call." Sabrina stepped back into the shadows. She had studied the layout of the garden and knew once she slipped between the hedges, he would lose her. She longed to continue this special moment, but she must leave.

His siren attempted to slip away. He must convince her to stay. "Who do you attempt to lure?"

The siren's laughter filled the garden as she slipped away. "Pirates. Who else?"

"Siren!" Graham called and followed her into the shadows. He ran along the hedge and around the fountain. She had disappeared before his very eyes.

Graham collapsed onto the bench. The scene before him had been as real as his dreams. Only this time, he actually had spoken to his mystery lady and held the taste of her still on his lips. While she had kept her face hidden and her hair colored differently, she hadn't been able to hide her eyes. They held the same soulful, mischief, and sadness as the lady he searched for everywhere. The same lady who haunted his dreams. Now that he had heard her lyrical voice, he was confident he would learn the identity of his siren soon.

And once he found her, he wouldn't let her slip from his grasp again.

Chapter Six

S ABRINA SNUCK INTO THE bedroom she had claimed as her
own for the duration of their stay. It was her own private
sanctuary where she hid from Lady Langdale. The lady never
bothered her unless she needed Sabrina to run an errand or to
make a demand for Sabrina to follow as she did this evening.
Lady L would expect a report on what Sabrina had learned
about the investigation.

However, Sabrina had found herself entranced by the
costumes once she set foot in the ballroom. Not long after her
arrival, Evelyn had latched onto her. When Graham captured
her attention in the garden, she had forgotten the reason for
her arrival at the ball. His charming nature and passionate
kisses had made her forget her mission for the evening.
Graham had become the only object of her attention. Even
when she escaped his clutches, he remained in her thoughts.
So much so she didn't return to the ball but wandered back
to the hideout, lost in her hazy memories of stolen kisses by a
dashing pirate.

She was a danger to herself. In her musings, she never paid
attention if anyone followed her. Anyone could've snatched
her, and she would've been powerless to stop them in the
contraption she wore. Sabrina smoothed her hands along the

dress. She remembered the gleam of male approval flashing in Graham's eyes when he stared at her. It was the exact spark she had hoped for.

She fell back on the bed, tracing her finger over her lips. The heat from his touch lingered and made her crave another kiss. If she snuck away to his home later, would she find him restless again, sitting on the balcony? Would he remember their kiss? Or was she another countless girl he kissed for his amusement? Sabrina wanted to believe he felt the same connection that sparked between them. But she wasn't sure.

The door to her room slammed open, and Lady L sauntered inside without Sabrina's permission to enter. But the lady thought since her coin paid the rent, she held free rein over the entire house. Sabrina leapt from the bed and pressed against the wall to prevent Lady L or her guards from sneaking up behind her.

"So you have returned. I've waited patiently for your visit to relay what you've learned this evening." Lady L walked up to Sabrina and brushed the hair off her shoulders.

"I wanted to change before I came to your bedchamber," Sabrina explained.

"I do not understand why you dislike dressing like a lady and insist on wearing the breeches of a boy. How will Graham Worthington ever fall for you if you dress like a heathen?" Lady L asked.

"I have no interest in Graham Worthington," Sabrina denied.

Lady L patted Sabrina's cheek. "Do not lie to your mother, Sabrina. A mother knows when her daughter has fallen in love. Also, when the gentleman has fallen smitten, too."

Sabrina brushed away Lady L's hand and growled. "You are not my mother."

"Am I not? My marriage to your father states otherwise," Barbara Langdale argued.

Sabrina gritted her teeth. She didn't want to ruin the wonderful memories of the evening over an argument they had had countless times before. "There is nothing to report. The investigation has come to a standstill. I never even heard your name whispered once all evening."

"Well, I cannot have that, can I? I must strike interest in my threats again. Perhaps I should start with blackmailing one of my victims." Lady L walked around the small room, plotting the next step in her revenge.

Sabrina waited for Lady L to leave, but it appeared her torment would continue.

"My sources informed me how you made some friends this evening. What is your opinion of Evelyn Worthington?" Lady L asked, her tone laced with malice.

Sabrina tensed. She should've been aware of the people Lady L sent to watch her every movement. She prayed Barbara hadn't learned of her time alone with Graham in the garden. "I apologize if it appears I betrayed you. I held no knowledge of who she was until she introduced herself this evening."

"Your lies are a waste of my time. I asked you what your opinion was of the lady Reese Worthington threw me over for. Now answer me," Lady L demanded.

"She was kind." Sabrina didn't elaborate with her description.

"Kind?" Lady L snarled. "Kind is how you describe an elderly matron. I cannot believe he does not stray. The Reese Worthington I remember had a healthy appetite between the bedsheets, one I am sure the current Lady Worthington doesn't appease. Well, she won't be an issue much longer and I will soon warm his bed again." A devious smile spread across her face.

Sabrina stayed silent. As much as she wished to learn more, she knew Barbara would only utter lies if she questioned her. She must listen in on Barbara's plans for revenge. Never had she mentioned getting rid of Evelyn Worthington. While she never stated she would kill the lady, Barbara implied the threat. She must alert her contact as soon as possible.

"You should build upon the friendship with the *kind* Evelyn," Barbara urged.

"I don't see how that is possible since Maggie and Noel will recognize me. Not to mention Dracott and Ravencroft will interfere," Sabrina argued.

"Mmm," Lady L murmured. "Yes. They are a threat to maneuver around. If anyone is capable of such, 'tis you, Sabrina. Make friends with her, and after you gain her trust, we shall lure her into a trap. Such a shame too on how she will meet an untimely death. Especially with another brat on the way. However, I will console Reese, and she'll become a forgotten memory."

Barbara Langdale had turned diabolical. Sabrina refused any involvement with these plans. She had gone along with the other plans because they never affected her and it helped her to gather the evidence she needed for Barbara's capture. But this threat indicated the power Barbara thought she held.

"Get your rest, my dear. There are plans you must set in motion tomorrow. Also, I need you to attend another ball tomorrow evening," Barbara ordered before leaving Sabrina alone with her thoughts.

Thoughts that kept growing more conflicted the more she attached herself to the Worthingtons. It was no longer her life on the line. It now involved Evelyn. Her only crime was how she had married the man she loved.

Sabrina only hoped she could stop Barbara Langdale in time.

Graham searched the gossip columns for any mention of his mystery lady. But nowhere did he find a name attached to a mermaid costume. The only piece he found was the question of who the enchanting creature might be.

Graham folded the paper and passed it over to his brother. At least not all his siblings were in attendance this morning, only the ones who resided in the townhome. Which left Maggie describing the ball to their mother, who at the last moment had stayed home with Reese and Evelyn's child, Mina. Her nanny had taken ill, and his mother hadn't wanted Evelyn to miss the entertainment.

"I met Evelyn's friend, and she wore the most spectacular costume of the evening," Maggie raved.

"Did you meet her too, Graham?" Lady Worthington asked.

"No, he didn't want to," Maggie answered for him.

Graham arched his eyebrow at his sister. "If I am not mistaken, I agreed. But it was Evelyn's friend who fled before I had the pleasure of meeting her."

Their mother seemed pleased with his answer to how he attempted to make the gentlemanly offer. But then his mother rarely found fault with him, much to his brother's and sisters' annoyance.

"And what was her costume, my dear?" Lady Worthington tried to distract Maggie away from harping on Graham.

"A mermaid. Her dress had colorful sequins decorating it all over, and she cut her skirt to look like a mermaid's tail. She told me she wore a wig and had painted it all the colors of the rainbow to match the dress. Oh, Mama, she was such a delight. We cannot wait for you to meet her," Maggie gushed.

Graham froze. He dropped the spoon he used to stir the honey and sugar around in the teacup. The *pretty* girl they wanted to introduce him to was his siren. Pretty was too tame of a word to describe the beauty who captivated him. The kisses they shared still lingered on his lips.

Lady Worthington smiled. "Does this lovely girl have a name?"

Lovely still didn't even come close to describing the graceful flow of her movements. The soft moans she released from his kisses. The husky softness of her laughter when she whispered how about she captured pirates.

"Sabrina Lancaster. I'm hoping she will attend this evening's ball," Evelyn answered.

"Sabrina Lancaster," Graham muttered under his breath. Sabrina. A fitting name for his siren.

"Did you say something, dear?" Lady Worthington asked.

Graham cleared his throat. "No, Mother. Just reminding myself of an appointment I must leave for."

Lady Worthington frowned at him. "I thought you mentioned you would clean your face after the costume ball."

Graham rubbed his hands across his cheeks, remembering how Sabrina had caressed him. He smiled. "That was until the ladies offered their compliments about how attractive they found this look on me."

Reese harrumphed. "I can only imagine which ladies those might be."

"Reese Worthington!" Lady Worthington reprimanded. "We do not discuss those topics at the table. Or ever, for that matter."

Reese glared at Graham, who smirked at him for getting reprimanded by their mother, still at his age and married no less. "My apologies, Mother."

"Maggie, where is Dracott?" Graham asked.

"At the office. He mentioned he might have a lead to follow up on." Maggie took a sip of her tea.

"Excellent. I will catch him there." He rose to kiss his mother and told everyone his goodbyes.

Now he had a name for Dracott to use in his search for the girl. Ever since he saw the flash of the multicolored dress last night, his luck had kept improving. Soon she would have nowhere to run.

But into his arms.

Chapter Seven

"W E HAVE TO TELL him," Ravencroft demanded.
Dracott glanced along the hallway in the office building before shutting the door. "We are not even sure if it was her."

"Why else did she flee, if it wasn't her?" Ravencroft argued.

Dracott sat down behind his desk. This wasn't a conversation he wanted to have with his brother, but Ravencroft wouldn't relent on his argument. He had never trusted Sabrina and probably never would, whereas Dracott still trusted her. He understood what she hoped to accomplish. However, her latest actions didn't sit well with him.

"Perhaps she was a nervous girl who fled because she feared Worth's rejection."

Ravencroft scoffed. "Who also holds the same name as Sabrina Lancaster?"

Dracott winced. Sabrina's actions had grown sloppy of late, and uttering her name put her at risk. It only took one member of the ton to remember the baron's first wife's maiden name was Lancaster and they had a daughter named Sabrina. And when Sabrina's mother passed away, the baron had married Barbara, the current Lady Langdale. "She has been making mistakes recently."

"Oh, hell." Ravencroft planted his hands on Dracott's desk. "She is the girl who Worth chased because she stole his bag of coin."

"Yes."

Ravencroft started pacing back and forth in front of the desk. "Because of Sabrina, Worth lost the chance to learn where their hideout was located. She helped to aid that bitch. Your silence is a betrayal. Even after she tortured you and made Noel and I suffer, you stay silent. When will you stop putting that girl first? Maggie and her family should be your only priority."

Dracott leaned forward. "Because Ren is my family, too. She saved my life more than once before you came along. When I abandoned her by following you, I left her in a vulnerable position with no one left to protect her. I owe it to her to keep her secret until she accomplishes her mission."

Ravencroft stopped pacing. "It is a foolish mission and you know that. I understand your loyalty to her. I really do. But you must understand what she hopes to accomplish is foolish. Lady Langdale is too sharp and never makes mistakes. Ren's need for revenge will only get her killed. Or those we love."

Dracott struggled with Ren's actions. He understood his brother's reasoning, but he owed Ren the time she needed. However, she had placed a target on her head by becoming friends with Evelyn. He didn't understand her agenda with that action. He needed to convince Ravencroft to allow her the freedom to gather her evidence or at least give him a chance to secure Sabrina's safety.

"Let me try to convince her to let us help her," Dracott bargained.

Ravencroft shook his head. "You've been unsuccessful on that front before. She'll be even more adamant now. She has to realize how close we are to bringing Lady L down. Ren has grown desperate herself. Why else do you think she has placed herself in danger? She is pushing the limit with Lady Langdale, hoping the lady will crumble. And we both know she will not."

"Give me a few days to try. Then if I can't convince her, we will tell Worth everything."

"Tell Worth what?" Worth walked inside the office with Falcone following behind him.

Dracott shot his brother a look, begging him to stay silent.

"We learned information about how Lady L visited the tavern again last night," Ravencroft explained.

Dracott breathed a sigh of relief. He had bought Ren a few more days to accomplish her goal. If not, then he must betray their friendship once again if she refused his offer of help. Finding her would be easy. To convince her to leave was one she would refuse.

Worth rubbed his hands together. "Ah, gentlemen, our luck has taken a turn for the better. We are close to capturing Lady Langdale. 'Tis only a matter of time."

Ravencroft looked at his brother in disappointment. "Yes, it might be. If only we held information on a key piece to help us break this case wide open."

Worth slapped Ravencroft on the back. "Soon, my friend, we will hold all the keys. In the meantime, Falcone and I will watch the tavern for any signs of our friend."

Dracott stood, sliding on his suit coat. "I will join you."

Worth shook his head. "No. I have another task for you."

Dracott frowned. "What might that be?"

"I have learned the name of my mystery lady. Your task is to discover whatever you can about her. Her name is Sabrina Lancaster."

"Is she not the lady the girls tried introducing you to last night?" Falcone asked.

"Yes. I've searched for this girl for weeks. At the ball, I followed a mermaid into the garden, and much to my surprise, it was her. She might have worn a mask, but I believe she is the same lady. Then when Maggie revealed her name at breakfast, I knew fate guided me to her," Worth explained.

"I will see what I can discover," Dracott said.

"Excellent. Come on, Falcone, let's follow Ravencroft's lead." Worth left, followed by Falcone.

"You have to the end of the week to convince Ren to leave Lady Langdale's clutches. If she refuses, then she leaves us with no other option than to save her." Ravencroft issued his ultimatum before leaving.

Dracott threw his head back against the chair. The task his brother set for him would be near impossible to accomplish. But he must try. He couldn't risk locating her today without Worth and Falcone questioning his appearance during their watch. He thought his deceit had ended when he married Maggie. But he had fooled himself.

It would never end until the truth told its own story.

"Do you believe in fate?" Worth asked Falcone.

Falcone gave Worth a peculiar look before staring out the carriage window again. "If you would've asked me that question a few months ago, I would've told you no."

"And now?"

Falcone rubbed at his shoulder. "My answer is yes. I ignored fate's nudging since I met Eden. But once I accepted my destiny, I allowed fate to guide me along my journey."

Worth smirked. "Deep, Falcone."

Falcone glared at Worth. "You asked."

"My apologies. I should not have mocked you and Eden. I am only curious."

"Did fate play a part with your mystery lady?" Falcone asked.

Worth flicked the curtain open wide to search the crowd. "Yes, I believe it did."

Falcone didn't comment. What could he say to Worth, other than he sensed the situation seemed peculiar? Why would a girl flee from an introduction, only to share a rendezvous with the gentleman in the garden? Also, the name Sabrina Lancaster seemed familiar to him. Perhaps if he saw the girl for himself, she might spark a memory to the connection.

Falcone blinked at the figure leaving the tavern. He hadn't seen this lady since he trailed Lady Langdale when she escaped to France after her exile. For days, he had followed her. Then she had disappeared along with Lady Langdale. Why did she return now?

"It cannot be her," Falcone muttered.

Worth sat forward, peering out the window. "Who? Lady Langdale?"

"No. There." Falcone pointed at the dowdy lady carrying a valise. "Do you see the lady walking behind those gentlemen?" They walked in their direction. Soon he would have a clear view of her.

"Yes. Who is she?"

Falcone's finger tapped on the window in his impatience for her to draw nearer. "At one time, she was Lady L.'s companion. I haven't seen her in years. I assumed she left the organization. But it appears she hasn't."

"I remember you mentioning a homely companion. Are you sure this is her?" Worth asked.

Falcone stared at the lady as she passed the carriage. "Positive."

"Maybe she will lead us to Lady Langdale." Worth opened the carriage door and leapt out.

"We should hang back and not get too close," Falcone warned.

Worth nodded in understanding, and they took off after Lady L's accomplice. After they walked along the road, the crowd surrounding them thinned out the closer they drew to the housing units set on the edge of town. Worth felt in his gut they would find where Lady L hid today. When she entered a storefront, Worth signaled for Falcone to wait while he followed the lady inside.

However, when he entered the storefront, the shopkeeper distracted his search by hovering by his side, asking him if he needed assistance. "What are you searching for? Perhaps a hair ribbon for a girl you hold a tender for."

The store was a mess, with merchandise scattered on tables and boxes stacked everywhere. "Did you see a lady walk in?"

The shopkeeper shook his head. "No, I did not. But we can ask the missus." The man cupped his hands around his mouth. "Mrs. Fitzgerald!"

Worth covered his ears at the maddening shout. The shopkeeper trapped him in the corner with no escape. He tried to scan the shop from where he stood, but it was no use. Worth had never visited a store this disorganized in his life.

"Yes, Mr. Fitzgerald," the wife yelled back.

"Are you by chance helping a lady?" Mr. Fitzgerald shouted.

"Perhaps we should find your wife for this conversation," Worth suggested.

"No. Only Ren. He needed a few items for his stepmother," Mrs. Fitzgerald replied.

"Pshh, there ain't no motherly bone in that woman's body. That lad would fare better living on the streets," Mr. Fitzgerald muttered under his breath.

"Do you perhaps have a back entrance?" Worth asked.

"Sure do," Mr. Fitzgerald answered with a smile on his face, rocking back and forth on his heels.

Worth bit back his growl of frustration. "Can you show me where?"

The shopkeeper turned and started along the aisle. He trudged along as he led Worth to the back, pausing to straighten the merchandise. It appeared as if Mr. Fitzgerald stalled for time. Once they reached the back door, Worth swore under his breath. A lady would've found it impossible to escape, considering the stack of boxes spread everywhere.

The bells chimed by the door, indicating someone had either left or entered. Worth's change of luck turned out of his favor once again.

"Mr. Fitzgerald, why are you showing a customer our storage room?" An older lady limped toward them, holding a cane for assistance. Every step seemed to trouble her.

"He asked if we had a back door, Mrs. Fitzgerald."

"Why?" she asked.

Mr. Fitzgerald shrugged. "You know I don't question when these toffs ask unusual questions."

Mrs. Fitzgerald shook her head. "How may we help you, sir?"

"I saw my mother's friend enter the store and wanted to offer to carry her purchases home." The lie slid easily off his tongue.

"Why, aren't you a gentleman?" Mrs. Fitzgerald complimented. "But I am afraid another customer occupied my attention, and I never saw a lady enter the shop."

"My mistake. I shall not trouble you any longer. Have a good day." Worth tipped his hat and walked toward the door.

But the sparkling color bouncing off the wall caught his eye. He moved toward the source. A variety of hair clips covered in sequins rested in a basket. He grabbed one and retraced his steps back to the Fitzgeralds. "Did you sell any of these to a young lady recently? She would have had raven-black hair and moved like a dancer."

"We only received those in today," Mrs. Fitzgerald informed him.

"Would you like to purchase one for your sweetheart?" Mr. Fitzgerald continued with his sales pitch.

Mrs. Fitzgerald avoided making eye contact with Worth and bustled around, pretending to organize the shop. She lied. However, Worth realized she would never admit the truth, no matter how much he pressured her. Just as she covered for the older lady who entered the shop but disappeared to the unknown. She would continue to lie about the girl who had bought the hair clips to decorate her hair.

"Yes. I shall purchase this one," Worth answered. He hoped his show of making a purchase and how he stopped asking questions would be taken as a sign they could trust him. He would return another day to seek the answers to the questions that plagued him, as soon as he started fitting the pieces of this puzzle into place.

"Excellent. Would you like me to wrap your purchase?" Mr. Fitzgerald asked.

"No need." Worth flipped a coin onto the counter and slid the clip inside the pocket of his suit coat.

As he exited the store, he decided not to question the Fitzgeralds about the valise sitting on the counter by the cash register. The same one the lady had carried into the store. As he stepped outside, Worth searched the area for any clue to help him solve this mystery.

Falcone came up next to him. "Is she in there?"

Worth shook his head. "If so, they hid her. Who left the store?"

"Just a boy wearing a cap. He carried a bundle out with him. I assumed some lad shopping for his mother," Falcone explained.

"Which direction did he go?" It was a pointless question, but one he wanted to ask anyway.

Falcone shrugged. "I didn't pay attention. Why?"

"I think the lady we searched for changed her clothes and made her escape right under our noses." Worth strode toward the carriage.

Falcone swore. "Damn. The lad was within my grasp."

"You mean the lass," Worth confessed after he settled in his seat.

Falcone grabbed the strap so his sore shoulder didn't slam into the wall when the carriage took off. "Do you believe it to be the same lass you chased the other day? It would make sense since you were about to learn information on Lady L's hideout."

"Yes. Do you remember of such a girl within Lady L's organization?" Worth inquired.

"No. However, there was another lad who followed Dracott around. I never paid much attention to him because Lady L never involved the lad with any of her crimes," Falcone explained.

"Because the girl constantly changed disguises. They led you and everyone else they conned into believing she was a different person. This girl is the key to helping us unlock this mystery," Worth declared. He withheld the information about the hair clip. He didn't want anyone to learn what he suspected until he found the girl on his own.

"It is urgent that we talk to Dracott and Ravencroft to learn more about her," Falcone said.

"I must find her," Worth whispered.

Chapter Eight

SABRINA TOOK A DEEP breath and smoothed her hand along her skirt before stepping out of the alcove. After her torturous day, she wanted to hide in the sanctuary she had carved for herself to escape from what Lady Langdale demanded of her, not attend another ball. But if she stayed, then she put herself at the mercy of the lady's wrath. Barbara had made her threats quite clear before Sabrina left. Sabrina must form a bond of friendship with Evelyn Worthington and arrange for them to meet outside of the Worthington townhome. Or else Barbara would allow her favorite guard the pleasure of tormenting Sabrina until she obeyed Barbara's orders.

Sabrina shuddered at what the torment would consist of. She had suffered from the guard's fists countless times before. But of late, the guard had expressed the nefarious and lewd acts he wish to torment her with. Sabrina shuddered at what he had planned for her.

She had no other choice. Sabrina must pretend to lure Evelyn Worthington into Barbara's clutches. In the meantime, she would find her contact and relay the new plan. She only hoped Evelyn stayed protected. She must return to the hideout even though she wished to avoid the place. To end this nightmare, she needed to finish gathering the evidence to bring about Barbara Langdale's demise. Sabrina only prayed the news she brought home would satisfy Barbara and keep the guard at bay. Then she must follow Dracott's advice and run fast and far away.

Sabrina watched as Lord Worthington stepped away from his wife. Evelyn smiled over his departure and started toward the area where Sabrina kept hidden. While glancing around, Sabrina made sure none of Evelyn's family was nearby. She pretended to stumble and bumped against Evelyn as she walked by.

"Oh, please excuse me," Sabrina exclaimed, clutching at the lady so she wouldn't fall.

Evelyn regained her balance. "Quite all right. I am unharmed." She looked up and saw Sabrina. "What a delightful surprise."

Sabrina smiled. "It has ended up as so."

"I apologize if my family scared you away last night," Evelyn explained.

"No. I am the one who must apologize. I feared my nerves overcame me at meeting someone as dashing as your brother-in-law." Sabrina tried to convince herself it wasn't a lie. Perhaps just embellished a bit.

Evelyn laughed. "Usually we must handle the opposite effect where Graham is concerned."

Sabrina attempted a smile. "I am sure the ladies flock around him."

Evelyn hooked her arms through Sabrina's and started them walking around the ballroom. "That is putting it mildly. But of late, his fascination with some mystery lady has him balking at every attempt we make in our introductions."

"She must hold a special place in his heart," Sabrina commented.

Evelyn smiled at her new friend. "Yes, I am sure of it. Now enough about Graham. Before I lose you again, I have a request to make." Evelyn stopped them near the refreshment table.

"And that may be?" Sabrina asked.

"May we meet outside of these functions? Perhaps for tea to become better acquainted. I promise not to force you into any more introductions."

Sabrina nodded. "I would love to."

Evelyn squeezed Sabrina's arm. "Excellent. How does Friday sound? There is a new tea shoppe in Mayfair I hear is all the rage."

"The Tea and Crumpet?" Sabrina asked.

"Yes, that is the one. Can we meet, say, about two o'clock?" Evelyn inquired.

"Sounds lovely," Sabrina answered.

Evelyn's eyes lit up when she saw her husband approach them. "Oh, this is even more wonderful. Reese, darling, this is my new friend Sabrina Lancaster I told you about."

Sabrina tensed when she turned around. Lord Worthington and Lord and Lady Falcone approached them. She prayed neither gentleman recognized her. While it had been a few years since she had seen Lord Worthington, she held a memorable experience from their visit. She crossed her fingers behind her back that he didn't remember her connection to Barbara.

Lord Worthington wrapped his arm around Evelyn and gave Sabrina a pleasant expression at meeting his wife's friend. "Miss Lancaster, it is a delight to make your acquaintance. Have you visited London before?"

Sabrina gripped her hands together to keep them from trembling. "It is a pleasure to meet you, too. Actually, I used to live in London. However, after my parents passed away, my guardian moved us to the Continent to live."

Sabrina didn't know if it was Worthington's formidable appearance or the fear of how she wouldn't be convincing with her lies at why she spoke too close to the truth. She had learned to speak as truthfully as she could, so she never got caught in her lies. But her confession didn't hold an ounce of a lie to keep them in the dark.

Eden laid her hand on Sabrina's arm in an act of sympathy. "You poor dear. How horrid for you to experience such losses at a young age. We must introduce you to our mother. She will gladly take you under her wing."

Sabrina smiled at Eden. "That is kind of you. I would enjoy meeting your mother. However, I no longer suffer from my losses but have learned to adapt to whatever circumstances come my way."

"Well, you shall no longer be lonely. You have us for friends now," Eden reassured Sabrina.

"Thank you, my lady," Sabrina answered.

Eden shook her head. "No 'my lady' between friends. Please call me Eden. And allow me to introduce you to my husband, Victor."

"A pleasure, Miss Lancaster. Where about on the Continent did you reside? I've spent much time abroad during the last few years," Lord Falcone asked.

Sabrina knew firsthand about his visits abroad, considering how his focus had been on trailing her activities. He was a hard man to shake. It wasn't until they left France that Sabrina could relax. That was, until he had found them again. However, by then Dracott had shown her how to hide her identity in a better disguise.

"We never stayed in one particular country. Our travels were quite sporadic. It is nice to settle in one place for a while," Sabrina explained.

Falcone nodded. "I can understand that. I would enjoy hearing more of your travels at a later time. Perhaps we can exchange stories of the different cultures."

Sabrina pasted on what she hoped was a smile, showing her interest. "I look forward to such a visit." She noticed her contact standing near the terrace doors. "If you will excuse me, there is someone I must speak to."

"Of course, dear. We did not mean to monopolize all your time this evening," Evelyn said.

Sabrina nodded and slipped away. The farther her steps took her away from them, the more her fear subsided. She had fulfilled Barbara's order by befriending Evelyn. The arranged meeting should pacify her stepmother, and it allowed Sabrina to place precautions to protect Evelyn.

Sabrina stopped in the terrace doorway. The cool breeze drifting in soothed her frazzled emotions. "I love evenings where the weather offers us relief from the heat of the day."

The older gentleman who stood nearby glanced over at Sabrina. "Yes, the heat has been quite stifling of late. I wonder how long this relief will last before the weather strikes with its next storm?"

"I fear one is to strike on Friday. One most ferocious could strike one you love most dearly," Sabrina replied.

The older gentleman narrowed his gaze on Sabrina before it trailed over to the guests Sabrina had just left. "Evelyn," he whispered.

Sabrina swallowed back the emotions she barely kept at bay and nodded.

"You must leave, Sabrina. If she is making threats at this level, then you are no longer safe. She is setting you up to take the fall."

"I cannot. I must stay until I secure the information I need," Sabrina told him.

He gripped at her hands, pulling her outside. "You must. I beg of you to leave. I will protect you at Colebourne Manor. It is where you should've lived after your father died. What I've asked you to sacrifice has been unfair. Please allow me to redeem myself. I could not bear it if something happened to you."

Sabrina kissed his cheek. "You haven't requested anything of me I've not wanted to do myself. Thank you for your guidance, Your Grace. Please keep Evelyn protected while I finish my assignment. I will be in touch soon."

Sabrina didn't give the Duke of Colebourne another chance to persuade her to stay with him. She slipped down the terrace stairs and hesitated on the last step. Part of her desired to steal back up the stairs and rejoin the party, hoping for a chance to see Graham Worthington. But the logical side urged her to make her escape. The sooner she gave Barbara the news, the less she had to worry about the guard tormenting her.

Perhaps one day she could give in to her curiosity. Just not today.

Graham had searched everywhere for a sign of Sabrina but found not one trace of her anywhere. He noticed his family standing near the dance floor and strolled their way. Perhaps Evelyn or Eden had talked to Sabrina this evening.

"How did you meet her?" Graham overheard Reese asking Evelyn.

"At the Kendrick Ball," Evelyn answered. "I wasn't feeling well so I rested in their library. She was taking a rest there too. So we struck up a conversation about the books we had read and other activities we enjoyed. It felt like I've known her forever. Why? Do you not like her?"

"She seems like a sweet girl, my dear. I only ask questions because I am leery of anyone new we meet. Also, there is something familiar about the girl I cannot quite place. I believe I might have met her at one time, years ago, when she was younger," Reese explained.

Eden scoffed. "I believe we are safe from Sabrina, dear brother. She appears harmless to me."

"Sometimes the most harmless of people are the ones we must protect ourselves from the most," Falcone warned.

Eden laid her head on her husband's arm. "I understand, my dear. I am only stating how I don't believe Sabrina means us any harm."

"Sabrina? Your friend is here this evening? I would like to meet her," Graham asked.

"I am afraid you missed her." Reese peered at his brother in suspicion for wanting to meet a girl he had tried to avoid the previous evening.

"Oh, that is a shame. Is she wearing a memorable dress again this evening?" Graham persisted.

Eden peered at her brother in confusion. "Sabrina wears a gown appropriate for the ball. Why the sudden interest?"

Graham shrugged, searching for any sign of her nearby. "No reason. I only wondered if she wore a dress that stood out in the crowd. Then I might find her and introduce myself."

"That would be most improper," Reese reprimanded Graham.

Graham rolled his eyes but didn't reply. Then his gaze landed on a lady who might be Sabrina. A lady with dark locks stood next to Colebourne by the terrace doors. They had their backs turned to the crowd and stared outdoors. Was it Sabrina?

"Evelyn, who is your uncle talking to near the terrace?" He pointed in their direction.

Evelyn stood on her tiptoes to see over the crowd. "Why, Uncle Theo is talking to Sabrina." She shook her head, smiling. "He is probably charming her to see if he can play matchmaker."

Graham arched his eyebrow at Reese. "Is it acceptable for Colebourne to introduce me to Sabrina if I wander over to them?"

Reese waved his hand for Graham to proceed. "Far be it from me to stop you from making a fool of yourself."

Graham smiled with confidence. "But we both know I won't. I will have her charmed before I even say a word to her."

"Conceited arse," Reese mumbled as Graham passed him.

He may be, but it was all a front in his family's presence. In actuality, he was worried he might scare her away. A swell of dancers finished their dance and prevented him from reaching Colebourne before Sabrina left. When he reached the duke, he found him standing alone.

"Did you scare her off with your matchmaking attempts?" Worth quipped.

Colebourne frowned. "Who?"

"The lovely girl you were speaking to," Worth explained.

"Ah, yes. She was quite lovely in all aspects. Very beautiful to gaze upon and had the sweetest voice. Not to mention her patience at talking with an old gentleman," Colebourne said.

"And here I hurried to your side, hoping for an introduction. You didn't see where she might have gone?" Graham continued his search amongst the crowd. At least now he knew the color and style of her dress.

Colebourne studied Graham. "So a glance across a ballroom floor has you smitten enough to forget all protocols of how a gentleman must behave?"

It wasn't so much a question but the duke's observation. If he pointed Graham toward where Sabrina fled, it would either lead Graham into danger or it held the possibility of Graham leading Sabrina out of danger. At this point, neither of them achieved the results they wanted in destroying Lady Langdale. Perhaps if they worked together, it would open them to more possibilities.

"What can I say? I am quite enamored with the lady," Graham replied.

"Mmm. I might have seen her slip into the garden," Colcbourne whispered.

Graham patted the duke on his back. "I owe you one."

He didn't wait to hear the duke's reply but ran down the stairs and started his search for Sabrina in the garden. His siren seemed to prefer the gardens over the ballroom floors.

Colebourne watched the young man chase after the damsel who was under more distress than she realized with the warning she gave him this evening.

"And I plan to collect it soon," Colebourne murmured before striding over to Worthington and Falcone.

"Uncle Theo, we hope Graham did not bother you too much. Please tell us what Sabrina's reaction was to his charm." Evelyn kissed her uncle's cheek.

"He missed her. She had already slipped away by the time he made it to my side," Colebourne explained.

Worthington laughed. "Serves him right."

Evelyn frowned at her husband. "We are on our way to dinner. Will you join us?"

Colebourne patted Evelyn's hand. "I would love to, my dear. Why don't you and Eden find us a table? I have something I must discuss with Worthington and Falcone. We shall be along shortly."

Evelyn gave them all a pointed look. "All right. But no talk of you-know-who."

"Of course. Just an issue with a bill in Parliament I need to discuss," Colebourne assured his niece.

Evelyn nodded, hooking her arms through Eden's as they walked toward the dining area. Colebourne motioned for Worthington and Falcone to follow him out to the terrace.

"Who is she?" Worthington demanded.

Colebourne grimaced. "She is one of my deepest regrets in life."

"She works for Lady Langdale," Falcone stated.

"No!" Colebourne growled his denial. "She is but a victim. A prisoner to Lady Langdale's whims and revenge."

Falcone leaned against the balustrade. "Who also works for you."

Colebourne sighed. "Aye."

"You never answered my question. Who is she?" Worthington asked again.

"If you search through your memory long enough, you will discover who she is. After all, you met her a few times while you carried on an affair with Lady Langdale," Colebourne answered.

Worthington closed his eyes once he remembered. When he opened them again, Colebourne was nodding his head in regret. "She is not Sabrina Lancaster but Sabrina Langdale. Barbara is her stepmother. I forgot about the girl."

"Lancaster was her mother's maiden name. Sabrina is a forgotten soul who no one thought to save," Colebourne stated.

"We need to protect her. Where did she go?" Falcone asked.

Colebourne tapped his cane on the ground. "Not tonight."

"Yes, tonight. Before Graham gets any more involved with the girl," Worthington demanded.

"Soon. Now we must join the ladies for dinner. Can you arrange a meeting tomorrow with Ralston, Kincaid, Dracott, and Ravencroft?" Colebourne asked.

"What about Graham?" Falcone inquired.

Colebourne shook his head. "His emotions are too fresh for the girl for what I must reveal. It is in his best interest to keep him in the dark until Dracott can pull the girl out safely."

"I disagree," Falcone argued. "Further involvement with this girl will only put him at risk."

"After we discuss this in further detail tomorrow, we can decide what course of action to take," Colebourne decided.

Worthington looked up at the sky before replying. "I will get Mother to occupy Graham."

"Let us join the ladies for dinner, gentlemen." Colebourne strolled inside.

"I do not like this," Falcone murmured low enough only for Worthington to hear him.

"I don't either. But you, more than anyone, understand how Colebourne holds all the cards. We can only pray he holds the winning hand," Worthington stated before they followed Colebourne into dinner.

If not, then they would all lose.

Chapter Nine

G RAHAM RUSHED ALONG THE garden path, hoping Sabrina hadn't disappeared again. He passed a few couples as they took a stroll, enjoying the cool breeze from the stifling air of the ballroom. But she wasn't amongst them. He tugged at his cravat in frustration. His steps led him to the center of the garden—and her. Sabrina. Her name fit her perfectly.

He stopped and gazed at her in silence. He didn't wish to break the spell surrounding her. She sat with her head tilted to the sky, with her eyes closed, and her lips lifted in a soft smile. His chest tightened as he watched her. Graham didn't know her story, but he sensed it was a sad tale filled with more heartache than she deserved. He only had to stare into her eyes to understand her suffering.

"I am beginning to think you have a fascination for gardens," Graham whispered.

Sabrina kept her head tilted; only she opened her eyes to see the stars sparkle down at her. They winked at her, telling her they had answered her wishes. "I find them a relaxing place to rest, surrounded by such beauty. The array of colors brightens the darkness that lurks inside one's soul."

Graham frowned. "That sounds meaningful, but I cannot believe an ounce of darkness resides in your soul."

Sabrina's lips pinched. "More than you might imagine."

Graham stepped forward and indicated if he may join her on the bench. When she nodded, he sat down, closer than he should have, but he couldn't resist the connection pulling him toward her. "Then perhaps I can shine some light into your soul."

Sabrina's smile lifted. "Do you think you are capable of such a task?"

Graham couldn't help himself. He leaned over and kissed Sabrina softly. "I am confident I can."

Sabrina touched her lips. "You are very presumptuous, sir."

Graham twirled a strand of her hair that escaped around his finger. "Perhaps. However, when I set my mind toward any task, I always achieve my expectations."

"Maybe I am the one you will fail at," Sabrina murmured.

Graham leaned over and stole another kiss, this one lasting longer. Sabrina's mouth opened under his with a soft moan. "I do not believe I will."

Sabrina shouldn't indulge in this interlude, but Graham was difficult to resist. It was why she waited on the bench, staring at the sky, and making wishes. She had hoped he would find her.

Graham brushed his thumb across her lips. "Will you at least give me a chance to try?"

Sabrina cupped his cheek, loving how the soft bristles caressed her palm. "I must warn you of the danger involved."

"I will face any danger for a chance to hold you in my arms," Graham declared.

"I've never even told you my name," Sabrina whispered.

Graham placed a hand over his heart. "My heart knows you as Siren. Any other name is just a name."

Graham knew who Sabrina was, and none of her past mattered to him in the slightest. To him, she was the other half of his soul. She wore the sins of her past as the scars of her survival. He only wanted to be the light who guided her out of the darkness. And he wanted her to hold the belief he would.

"My name is Sabrina." Sabrina wanted honesty between them in one detail of their time together.

"My name is Graham. My friends and family call me Worth."

"Graham."

"Will you come with me?" Graham stood up, holding out his hand.

Sabrina bit at her bottom lip, weighing the danger of following him. If Barbara learned of this stolen moment, she would include Graham in her plans with Evelyn. She argued with herself. If she didn't grab this opportunity, then she might never have another chance. As much as she wanted to steal a selfish moment for herself, she shouldn't. "I've been away from the ball too long as it is."

Graham slid his hand through his hair. "My apologies. It was improper for me to make such an offer. My only excuse is how I lose all common sense when I am around you."

Sabrina twisted the gloves in her lap. "You appear to know which charming words to speak to win a lady over. I can only assume you have had much practice in that regard."

Graham sat back on the bench and gathered her hands in his, rubbing her knuckles to calm her. "I will admit I have relied on my charm in the past to get my way. However, with you, I speak the words from my heart."

Sabrina stared into his eyes and saw the honesty of his words. Or what he believed to be true. Because the desire swirling around them kept tempting them to indulge in its heady power. "Still, I should return."

Graham heard the hesitation in her voice. "Of course. Your chaperone must wonder where you are."

"Doubtful," Sabrina muttered. "I mean, she entertains herself at these events, and I usually must find my own way home."

Sabrina cringed at telling Graham another lie. But if she agreed with his comment about returning to her chaperone, he would insist on meeting her. Yet another imaginary character she conjured to get out of the predicaments she kept placing herself in.

"Then perhaps you will allow me to escort you home," Graham suggested.

Sabrina took a deep breath, fighting off the panic attack ready to consume her. "No. No. It is unnecessary. Also, the servants would inform my chaperone of how I returned home. I do not wish to anger her."

It wasn't fair of Graham to keep pressuring Sabrina. He had pushed the issue, hoping she would confess her predicament to him. However, he had yet to gain her trust.

"Well, then may I propose an offer?"

Sabrina's gaze drifted to the ball, then back at Graham. She nodded.

Graham made another attempt to win her over. "Will you allow me to show you a place I hold dear to my heart? For only an hour. Then we will return and I will find you a safe ride home."

"Is it very far?" Sabrina asked. Her answer swayed to accept his offer.

A hopeful gleam lit Graham's eyes. "Only two blocks away. We can slip out the back gate and return before you know it."

Graham made it sound tempting and easy to escape without getting caught. Barbara wouldn't expect her to return this early. Also, Lady L's guards always kept to the front of the estate with their vigil to watch Sabrina's activities. "Can you make it possible for us to return in one hour?"

Graham tugged Sabrina to her feet. "I promise."

Sabrina's laughter trailed behind them as Graham hurried them toward the back gate. When they reached it, he searched the lane for any sign of anyone watching them. When he deemed them safe, he wrapped his arm around Sabrina's waist and urged her to their destination.

Graham's act of protecting her tugged on Sabrina's heartstrings. His arm wrapped around her gave her a sense of security she hadn't felt since her parents lived. Even with Dracott's protection all those years, she had still feared the unknown. Yet she hadn't known Graham for long and he wrapped her in layers of security by just being nearby.

Graham surprised Sabrina when he unhooked the gate leading to a small house nestled behind a larger townhome. She stayed silent until they were inside. "Where have you taken me?"

Graham moved around the room, lighting a few candles. The flickering light offered them a soft glow to show Sabrina they stood in what appeared to be a family room. Two chairs sat close to the fireplace, a row of bookcases filled with books lined a wall, and a sofa rested across from the chairs. Sabrina moved behind the sofa, and her fingers trailed over the blanket resting on the back. The room breathed a comfortable atmosphere to steal away and enjoy the simplicity of a normal life. One she hadn't experienced in forever and she didn't believe she would again.

"My home," Graham stated with pride.

"You live here?" Sabrina questioned.

Graham shrugged. "Sometimes. Only when I wish for a moment of peace from my family. It is a place I can call my own. Also, it helps me regain my sanity when needed."

Sabrina smiled in understanding at him. "Thank you for sharing your home with me. Whenever we move, I always claim a room for my sanctuary."

Sabrina didn't understand why she shared something so personal with him. Perhaps it was because he shared a part of himself with her. She wandered around, gazing at how the décor reflected his personality. Graham Worthington may appear a gentleman who used his charm to get by. However, he was really a simple gentleman who wished for the simplicity of life. A man Sabrina found harder to resist with each facet he showed her.

Graham came up next to her. "Will you sit with me?"

Sabrina nodded, and he guided them toward the sofa. When he sat down, he left no space between them. His arm rested on the back of the sofa behind her. She shifted her body so she could speak with him. But the look he held in his eyes held her spellbound. Shots of emeralds exploded from his gaze, each one displaying the need he held for her. Sabrina reached up to touch his cheek again.

"Are you still pretending to be a pirate?" Sabrina didn't recognize her husky whisper.

She melted at the smile he gifted her. It held a side of mischief, defiance, and desire in one simple act. She loved how his emeralds darkened to a lush green forest when she touched him. Sabrina lifted her other hand to cup his other cheek. When he growled his pleasure, the soft roar spread warmth through her soul.

"I kept my face this way because I enjoy how you rub your palms against my cheeks. Do you wish for me to shave?"

Sabrina shook her head slowly back and forth. "No. I crave how your whiskers scratch against me when you steal your kisses."

"Steal, huh?" Graham teased.

"Yes. I hear that is how one describes a pirate's actions," Sabrina teased in return.

"Well then, I must steal my bounty before my time slips away."

Graham drew Sabrina into his embrace and ravished her as if he were a pirate. Each pull of his lips demanded for her to surrender to his advances. When her hands slid into his hair and tightened on his locks, he knew his captive was agreeable to his demands. His tongue coaxed her lips to open under his, and he swirled it around, savoring her exotic taste. It only left Graham craving the treasure of her sweetness.

His lips trailed a path along her neck, nipping and sucking on each delicious inch of her exposed skin. Sabrina arched her neck to give him better access. He needed no other encouragement to offer her pleasure. Graham trailed his fingers along her arm, down to where her hand rested on her stomach. He intertwined his fingers with hers and guided them up her chest and to her bosom. He whispered in her ear, "May I touch you here?"

Sabrina gifted Graham's request with a smile. "I thought a pirate only seized what he wanted."

Graham groaned. "Perhaps I ask as a gentleman."

Her smile turned so seductive it was practically wanton. "'Tis a shame then because I only desire for a pirate to discover my treasures."

Graham dropped her hand and raked his fingers into her hair, sending her pins scattering everywhere. "God, woman! Where have you been my entire life?"

His lips plundered hers, not waiting for a reply. It wasn't a question but a statement declaring how in awe he was of the effect she held over him. He stole whatever she gave him. Their lips locked in a kiss, declaring their every desire.

Graham's hand slipped back onto her breasts and teased her nipples until they poked through her dress.

He dipped his head and suckled on the buds through the fabric, while Sabrina held him to her, arching her chest to his mouth. Her whimpers declared her need was as strong as his. He never meant to take his seduction this far this evening. Graham only wanted to show her how much she could trust him with her secrets. But one kiss hadn't been enough for his greedy soul.

Sabrina ached for him to pull her gown down and fasten his lips around her nipples instead of teasing them through the thin material. Her body craved for Graham to stake his claim and make them one. Sabrina reached between them and tore at the bow that held the ribbon in place. Once it released, she tugged at the strings until her gown spread apart. The cool air washed over her skin, but it did nothing to aid the heat consuming her soul. Each brush of his bristled cheeks against her skin increased her need for him to possess her heart and soul.

"Please," Sabrina whimpered.

Graham fitted her exposed breast into his palm, and his tongue swirled around her nipple, teasing Sabrina with each lick. "Mmm. A pirate does not follow a captive's demands," he purred, and Sabrina whimpered again. "But perhaps I can make an exception with your plea since I ache to suck this sweet treasure between my lips."

Graham's mouth closed over Sabrina's nipple, melting her into the sofa with the gentle pressure. However, the pressure increased the harder he suckled the bud, causing a pool of warmth between her thighs. His lips tormented her with the aching pleasure as his bristled cheeks moved from one breast to the other, never relenting from her demands.

Sweet didn't even describe how Sabrina tasted. She was every exotic essence mixed into one exquisite flavor that was her alone. He wanted to savor every inch of her and memorize every silken limb of her entwined with him. He lifted his head to watch her reaction as he slid his hand up her dress and along her leg. Her eyes lifted, and she gazed at him with longing.

He promised to stop after one touch. Somehow, he must find the strength to part from her. The promise he made to return them to the ball drew near. Graham refused to betray her trust this early.

Please touch me, Sabrina silently begged, hoping he would ease the ache consuming her. She didn't want Graham to think her a hussy who had experience, but she wasn't naïve either. Because her stepmother forced her to witness her acts of depravity.

She closed her eyes at his first touch. His gentleness showed Sabrina she hadn't been mistaken about him. He fulfilled her every fantasy with his gentle care. His fingers glided along her softness, caressing her folds. When he slid a finger inside her, easing her tight core to loosen with each pull in and out, Sabrina clutched at his arms, afraid she had floated away.

He had lied. He couldn't stop at one touch, not when she spread her legs so trustingly and moaned with each stroke of his finger inside her. Her wet dew clung to his fingertips. He lowered his head again to suckle on her berries, while teasing her folds with his gentle touch. Graham hoped it would help appease his need, but the desire to sample her greatest treasure overcame him.

"Please," Sabrina whimpered again.

Graham fought against his own desires and stopped himself from settling between her thighs. They must return because her safety depended on it. He rested his head against her breasts, bringing his own fierce desire under control. Sabrina's fingers fluttered in his hair, and she pressed her core into his hand, making a silent demand. When he pulled his hand away, a moan filled with longing escaped from her lips.

Sabrina squeezed her eyes closed, fighting the waves of desire held at bay and demanding release. "You make for a horrible pirate, Graham."

Graham set to securing Sabrina's dress back into place. His fingers shook as he threaded the ribbon back through the eyeholes they had escaped from. He tied the bow and smoothed the skirts back down her legs. Once he properly covered her, he tugged her to a sitting position and kissed her lips softly.

Graham enclosed her in a hug. "On that, we will agree, Sabrina."

The clock started striking the hour. Once it struck the second hour, Sabrina pushed out of Graham's arms. She hadn't realized their time had surpassed the hour he promised her. She must return before the guards noticed her absence.

Graham watched Sabrina's panic grow, and it was all his fault. His greediness to steal away with her could cause dire consequences for her. He rose, blew out the candles, and guided Sabrina back to the ball. He never spoke a word, understanding how it would only intensify her worry. Graham fought to remain calm, battling his need to protect her. He didn't want to relinquish her to the horror she lived in.

Once they reached the terrace steps, he pulled her behind a bush and smoothed her hair away from her face. "Sabrina, I hope you can understand how you can trust me with your secrets. I will not judge you. I want to be the man you can lean on in your time of need."

Sabrina touched his cheek one last time. "As I said before, I only require a pirate at this time."

Before he responded, Sabrina slipped out of his grasp. She lifted her skirts and ran up the stairs. However, she gifted him with hope when she glanced at him over her shoulder before slipping into the ballroom. From there, he assumed she left the ball.

Graham lifted his hand to soak up the warmth from her touch. Her sweet fragrance drifted from his fingers. He inhaled the scent, breathing her into his soul. Graham brought his fingers to his mouth and licked off his fingers. "Then a pirate you shall get, my sweet siren."

Graham followed the trail around the townhome and leaned against the wall, waiting for Sabrina to leave. He didn't have to wait long before she rushed down the stairs. He kept close to the shadows, following her. However, she didn't stay alone for long before two brutes flanked her sides. One of them grabbed her arm and jerked her against him. Graham increased his pace, ready to defend her. But Sabrina kicked out her leg, forcing the brute to drop her. Sabrina sneered at him and offered her own threat. Of course she didn't intimidate either man, and they shoved her into a carriage.

Graham almost forced his way into the carriage but stopped when he saw Lady Langdale issuing her orders before the door closed. One guard joined the carriage driver, while the other one rode on the back to guard them.

Graham held back, keeping a notable distance between them. He stuck to the shadows and followed them on foot since other carriages filled the streets, slowing their progress. Since he heard no screams coming from the carriage, he assumed Lady Langdale didn't harm Sabrina.

The deeper they drove into the shadier section of London, near the docks, the more the carriage picked up a little speed. But with the around-the-clock activity of loading and unloading ships on the dock, their pace turned to a crawl again. Graham thought he might lose them when they entered a section of housing, but the carriage slowed to a stop.

Lady Langdale disembarked, dragging Sabrina behind her. Graham realized he had finally located the illustrious thief who had tormented his family over the past few months. He hated to, but he must leave Sabrina. He would return with the authorities and bring Barbara Langdale's reign of terror to an end.

And rescue Sabrina too.

Chapter Ten

SABRINA STARED OUT THE bedchamber window. She swallowed her gasp when she noticed movement across the street. She didn't have to strain her eyes to see Graham had followed them. Oh, what had she done? She never should have left with him this evening. Her actions only opened up a whole new set of problems.

Please leave. Please leave before they see you, she chanted to herself.

Barbara sneered. "After taking in your attire, I can understand why there was a delay on your return."

Sabrina turned, smoothing her hands along her skirt. "My delay was only with my attempts to secure your request."

Barbara narrowed her gaze, taking in Sabrina's disheveled hair and the wrinkles in her dress. "And did you?"

"Yes."

Barbara's lips turned into a smile, one Sabrina had learned never to trust. "Excellent. When and where?"

Sabrina dreaded telling her, but she had no other choice. "This Friday. I am to meet her for tea in Mayfair."

Barbara moved to the door. "You did very well this evening, and in more ways than one, it appears. I never could resist Reese's prowess, so I understand how you were powerless to resist Graham's pursuit. Much as you may dislike hearing this, you behave more like me with each passing day. I only hope he satisfied you in those few stolen moments. If not, then what a shame. You have earned yourself a reprieve from the guards for now. However, if you continue to stray without a care, then I will enjoy the guard's entertainments when I throw you into his lair," she warned before locking Sabrina into her bedchamber.

Sabrina blocked out Barbara's words. The lady knew which taunts to throw at Sabrina to make her question her every action. But Sabrina refused to give her that power anymore. She didn't feel an ounce of shame or remorse for the passion she shared with Graham. Sabrina treasured the beauty of their time together. She remembered his every word and action and allowed the memories to wrap her in the security he gifted her. His last words were a lure she must resist. However, they kept her heart warm.

She returned to the window, searching for him, but only found emptiness instead. He had left. Relief should wash over her at how he remained safe from the danger. Instead she suffered from the same abandonment as when Dracott left. Only Graham's departure affected her more deeply, and heartache overtook her.

Sabrina fell onto the bed, curled into a ball, and cried out her sorrow. She muffled her cries against the pillow so Barbara wouldn't take pleasure from her pain. Her tears streamed in endless paths down her cheeks, settling in the strands of her hair. Sabrina lifted her hands to her hair and realized that was how Barbara had guessed her tryst with Graham. She had forgotten he had dislodged her pins when he speared his hands through her hair to claim a kiss. She glanced down and saw the red scratches across her bosom where he had left his mark as he claimed his treasure. The reminder of their passion brought about a fresh wave of tears.

Sabrina had never felt more alone.

Worth dragged Ralston out of bed and brought him to the house where he had followed Sabrina. Darkness shrouded the house, and no men stood guard as they had earlier. They walked to the mews down the road, searching for their carriage and horse. But they had disappeared too.

"I'm telling you, I followed them here," Worth insisted.

Ralston sighed. "It may be so. They must have spotted you and fled. That house is empty."

Worth stormed across the road and threw the door open to the house. Just as Ralston suspected, they had fled, not leaving one piece of evidence behind.

"Damn! I was so close." Worth punched the wall.

His frustration wasn't only from not capturing Lady Langdale. Fear coursed through him at how he might've placed Sabrina in danger of leading him to their hideout. He flew up the stairs to the bedchamber where she had stared at him from the window.

It was empty except for a bed frame with a sagging mattress. No sign showed her presence, except for her fragrance that perfumed the air. He sat on the bed, staring out the window, and watched the sunrise.

"Where did you go?" Worth murmured.

A flash of color bounced off the floor and displayed on the wall when the sun hit it. He looked down and saw a sequined hair clip. It matched the clip on the inside of his pocket. He bent over, smiling at the clue she had left behind. They had the correct house, only he was too late to arrive.

"Perhaps you mistook which road you traveled upon. We can have Kincaid's men search the area," Ralston said, standing inside the doorway.

Worth's fingers closed over the hair clip. "No, I had the correct one. Perhaps it wouldn't hurt if they turned this house inside out. There must be clues somewhere to their activities."

Ralston cocked his eyebrow. "Can I return to my wife now?"

Worth grimaced. "It troubles me to have Gemma suffer from your company, but I suppose you can. If not, she might bar me from entering your home again."

"As if Gemma would dare hold a grievance against you. You are quite aware of the soft spot she holds for you," Ralston grumbled.

"Only because she was once my betrothed," Worth bragged, knowing how much his comment irritated his friend.

"You know damn well you were not," Ralston growled.

Worth chuckled. "It depends on whose matter of opinion you ask."

He looked over his shoulder as they left, hoping Sabrina would materialize out of thin air. However, only the empty house met his gaze. He regretted not storming the house. He might have met his demise, but at least he would have tried to save Sabrina. If luck prevailed and gave him another chance, he wouldn't hesitate.

But would he be so lucky?

He wanted to continue his search for Sabrina. Instead, Graham followed his mother into another shop. He still didn't understand how she had roped him into escorting her around town this morning. He had argued about his need to visit his office, but his mother had insisted for him to keep her company. Since the rest of his family made themselves scarce, he had grudgingly agreed.

Soon, the morning turned into the afternoon. His mother perused the shops with a slowness that drove him mad. Each of her purchases she pondered over with indecisiveness.

If his thoughts weren't so consumed with Sabrina, he would've realized how his mother stalled to keep him away from home. Since he never noticed her covert glances at her timepiece, he was clueless to her agenda.

Graham blew out a breath. He waited near the door, ready to leave as soon as his mother finished her browsing. He crossed his arms over his chest, drumming his fingers on his arms with impatience.

"Oh, dear. Please forgive my clumsiness." Lady Worthington held out her arm so the girl didn't knock over a display of ribbons.

"It is not your fault, my lady. It was I who didn't pay attention." The soft melody of the girl's voice shook Graham from his annoyance.

He turned around and saw his mother with her arm on Sabrina, so she didn't topple over. Sabrina's hands reached out to steady the ribbon holder. Graham rushed forward and helped her regain her balance. He closed his eyes for a brief moment, relieved at seeing her again. His mother cleared her throat, and her shrewd gaze looked at his hold on the girl.

Once Graham realized she wouldn't fall, he dropped his hands. Much to his misery, he stepped back. "Are you all right?"

Sabrina blushed at his bold attention. "Yes."

"It is a delight to see you again," Graham said. He couldn't tear his gaze away from her.

Sabrina tucked her hair behind her ear. "It is a pleasure to see you, too."

Lady Worthington pinched her son in the side to get his attention. "Since my son is lacking the manners I taught him, may I inquire to how you two became acquainted?"

Graham rubbed at his side but kept the foolish smile on his face. "Mother, please allow me to introduce you to Sabrina Lancaster. Sabrina, this is my mother, Lady Worthington."

Lady Worthington smiled with kindness at Sabrina. "Evelyn's friend. How wonderful to meet you. I can see why my son is so smitten. You are quite pretty."

"You are too kind, Lady Worthington." Sabrina risked a glance at Graham, then grimaced.

Lady Worthington looked between the two. "Did I say something wrong?"

Sabrina smiled with humor twinkling in her eyes at Graham, proving how she was more than simply pretty. She was gorgeous beyond any words to describe how so.

Sabrina lifted her gloved hand to hide her smile. "No. Only your son has expressed his aversion to someone described as pretty." Her voice dropped to a conspiratorial whisper. "Once he hears the description, he runs in the opposite direction."

Lady Worthington watched the display of humor between her son and this lovely girl. In all honesty, Sabrina was more than pretty, and her son remained rooted to her side. She didn't think he would run anywhere but into the girl's arms. Lady Worthington wanted to squeal at the attraction simmering between them. There was no worthier match for her son than the lady she had accidentally bumped into.

"Since I almost knocked you over, will you accept my forgiveness over a cup of tea? We have finished with our shopping, and I need a brief respite before I make the journey home. We would love if you would join us," Lady Worthington offered.

"Finally," Graham muttered.

Lady Worthington arched her eyebrow at her son. "Excuse me?"

"Nothing, Mother." He turned to Sabrina and winked. "Please say you will join us."

"How can I resist such a kind offer? I would love to," Sabrina agreed.

"Allow me a minute to make this purchase and we shall try the place next door." Lady Worthington walked over to the shopkeeper and handed over a bonnet she wished to purchase.

His mother left him alone with Sabrina, who turned her attention to the ribbons. She stepped forward to run her finger across a green ribbon with a rose pattern running down the middle. She bit at her bottom lip, and Graham saw the longing in her eyes. Her glance drifted to the front of the store after she drew her hand away and stepped back. His mother discussed with the shopkeeper where to have her purchase delivered.

Graham stepped forward and brushed his fingers against hers. She didn't pull away from him, and instead she opened her hand and faced her palm out to him. Even though they both wore gloves, the impact of touching each other still held a profound effect on him. The act itself communicated how much he wanted to touch her.

He wanted to question her about what had caused her disappearance. Where did they vanish to? Did she need his protection? However, he stayed silent. Because he didn't want to scare her away by revealing he had learned of her various identities and her connection to Lady Langdale.

"The ribbon would look pretty in your hair," Graham commented.

Sabrina twisted her lips and peeked at him out of the corner of her eye. "Pretty? I cannot tell if your compliment is offensive or not."

Graham laughed loudly enough to draw his mother's notice. "I meant no offense, my dear. I failed with my poor attempt to pay you a compliment. Allow me to rephrase that; the lovely shade of green will be a perfect adornment to wear within your glorious locks of hair."

Sabrina's eyes widened. "My dear?" she whispered.

Graham was powerless to look away from the mischief twinkling in her gaze. She teased him with ease, as if she had for years. She was beyond amazing. "My dear. My siren. There are many more endearments I wish to whisper in your ear. However, I shouldn't dare. Some are more scandalous than others."

He longed to whisper "my love." However, Sabrina wasn't ready to hear his declaration yet.

The blush heating Sabrina's cheeks didn't stop her from asking, "Why should you not dare?"

Graham chuckled. "For that reason alone. Now you will have to explain your blush to my mother."

Sabrina turned away from his mother, who was walking in their direction, and covered her cheeks. "You are a rascal, Graham Worthington."

Graham whispered, "I much prefer to be your pirate instead."

Sabrina gasped. "Oh."

"Are you ready, Sabrina? I hope Graham hasn't been too much of a bother," Lady Worthington inquired.

Sabrina peered at Graham with a serious expression before smiling at Lady Worthington. "Not too much where I couldn't manage him."

Lady Worthington laughed. "Oh, I think we shall get along fabulously."

Sabrina walked next to Lady Worthington as they headed out of the shop. She turned her head for one more glance at the ribbon before they left. Perhaps one day she could buy all the ribbons she wanted. But not today.

Lady Worthington kept up a steady flow of conversation until they settled at a table next door in a tea shoppe. Sabrina only held a few coins, and she prayed it was enough to cover the cost of a cup of tea.

"Now where did he wander off to?" Lady Worthington questioned, swiveling around to search the tea shoppe. "He complained all morning about escorting me around, and now that I've finished shopping, I cannot find him."

"Perhaps he found something he wished to purchase," Sabrina suggested.

"Well, here he comes now. We shall find out." Lady Worthington winked at Sabrina.

"My apologies, ladies. When I left the store, I noticed this doll for Mina. I do not believe she has one like this." Graham held up the doll he had purchased.

It was more of a rag doll with string hair and buttons for its facial features. The doll wore a medieval dress. It wasn't a doll someone would give their child in the aristocracy but more of a toy for the less fortunate. But none of that seemed to matter to Graham or Lady Worthington either.

"She will love it. You spoil her so." Lady Worthington patted Graham's hand. "Mina is Evelyn and Reese's daughter. She is a doll herself. We must have you over for tea so you can meet her."

Graham chuckled. "Beware, though, she has the ability to wrap everyone around her finger. None of us can resist her sweetness."

Lady Worthington joined in, laughing. "That she does."

Sabrina smiled. "She sounds lovely."

Graham placed their order. They enjoyed a pot of tea and slices of cake while they entertained Sabrina with stories of their family's antics. On Lady Worthington's every attempt to turn the conversation toward Sabrina to learn more about her, Graham swiftly regaled them with another humorous tale. She didn't understand why, but he held her gratitude for his interference.

"It was lovely to meet you, Sabrina. Do come for tea soon," Lady Worthington offered.

"I enjoyed meeting you, Lady Worthington," Sabrina said.

"Please call me Meredith."

Sabrina nodded. "Meredith. Thank you for tea, Mr. Worthington. It was most gallant of you."

Graham lifted Sabrina's hand and placed a kiss across her knuckles. "My pleasure."

Sabrina grew warm at Graham's bold act and knew a blush graced her cheeks in a flaming red color. In front of his mother, no less. The man held no shame. Yet she wouldn't complain too much because of how she craved any attention from him.

"May we give you a ride home?" Lady Worthington asked.

"Thank you, but no." Sabrina pointed across the street. Not to any shop in particular, but enough to make her excuse plausible. "I promised to meet my stepmother at her modiste."

When Sabrina lowered her arm, Graham bumped into her and knocked her reticule to the ground. "Allow me," he offered. He bent over to retrieve it and handed it to Sabrina. "Until we meet again."

Sabrina smiled and waved them off. She headed across the street in case they watched her. When she glanced back, they were nowhere to be found. She slipped around the corner and started walking back to their new hideout.

Along the way, she passed a park and found a bench to sit upon as she thought about her visit with Graham and Lady Worthington. It was a pleasant afternoon, one she hadn't experienced since her father was alive. But even those visits had been fraught with the unexpected because of his irregular behavior. Her life hadn't resembled normal since her mother was alive. She had been their rock and knew how to manage her father's behavior. Once her mother died, Sabrina's life had been an uphill battle with every step a fight to take.

She longed for the simplicity of life but didn't believe she could function with normal. Sabrina had spied on Dracott since his marriage to Maggie Worthington, and he appeared as if he had adapted quite well. Dracott no longer wore deep shadows under his eyes from his restless nights. She wondered if the night terrors that plagued him had ceased.

That was how she passed her days away, unless she had to follow Barbara's bidding. She spied on Dracott, Ravencroft, and sometimes Rogers, the Worthingtons' butler. Everyone she had relied on once upon a time. They had escaped Barbara's clutches and made fresh starts. As much as she wanted to leave, she must remain until she found the last piece to destroy Barbara Langdale.

Sabrina rubbed her arm in a gentle caress. The tenderness still lingered from where Barbara had dragged her out of bed while she slept. She had raged and accused Sabrina of leading Graham back to their hideout. That if she hadn't trifled with him, then he would've never thought to follow her. She told Sabrina how Graham must have discovered who she was. But Sabrina had denied the accusation. He had never spoken a word to Sabrina that revealed he had discovered her true identity.

But yet in a way he had. He told her how she could trust him to help her. Sabrina shook her head. Nonsense. He only made the statement because she acted skittish and uncertain whenever he asked about her past. Also, how she made excuses to avoid any meetings.

When she awoke this morning and found the house empty except for the lady who owned the home, Sabrina had left and walked to the shopping district, wanting to pretend to be a normal lady who passed the day away with shopping. Even though she only held a few coins to her name. Coming across Graham and his mother had been a coincidence, unlike the other moments where she had made it a point to cross paths with him or his family.

She smiled as she remembered how she teased him and how he returned her teases in a familiar manner. He was unlike anyone she had ever met. His laid-back manner quieted her soul. Yet whenever he touched her, he sent her emotions ricocheting all over the place.

She shouldn't linger any longer. Sabrina grabbed her reticule and frowned when the clasp wouldn't close. She opened the bag and found the green ribbon decorated with roses inside. Sabrina pulled the ribbon out and held it in her palm.

Graham.

He must have purchased it for her and knew how much she would've refused his generous offer. So he snuck it into her bag to find later. The sneaky devil.

Graham's gift was an endearing gesture, showing Sabrina how thoughtful he was. She feared she only fell deeper for him. At first, he had fascinated her, and she had held a small crush on him. However, once she met him and spent time alone with him, her feelings had turned from simple infatuation to love. What other word was there to describe the emotions he invoked with the attention he gave her? She had never meant to fall in love and held no clue what to do. Her emotions conflicted with the plans she had and left her in doubt about why she remained.

Sabrina looked around her and noticed she sat alone in the park. She raised her skirts and quickly tied the ribbon above her knee, then stood up. She couldn't afford for Lady L to see the gift. It wouldn't do to anger her stepmother any more than her absence probably had.

Which left Sabrina wondering, was it all even worth it anymore?

Chapter Eleven

"WHERE IS ROGERS?" WORTH asked as he carried his mother's packages inside later that day. The butler never opened the door to greet them.

Lady Worthington took off her gloves and bonnet. "Perhaps he took the afternoon off."

Worth frowned. "It appears even the servants, as well as our family, made themselves scarce today. I wonder why?"

Lady Worthington walked toward the parlor, hoping her son would follow her. "Who knows with them? Come sit with me. I wish to hear more about Sabrina. I noticed how smitten you are with her."

Worth smiled at hearing Sabrina's name. He realized his mother wouldn't relent until he answered her countless questions of how he felt about Sabrina. Worth decided to pacify her and entered the parlor. However, he stopped when he heard raised voices coming from Reese's study. Then a door slammed. He stepped back into the hallway and saw Charlie, Evelyn's sister, and her husband, Jasper Sinclair, whispering in disagreement.

"Just a minute, Mother." He strode along the hallway toward the Sinclairs.

"I will not allow it," Sinclair hissed.

Charlie ran her hands up and down his arm. "Let us listen to their plan. We do not have to agree if it sounds too dangerous."

"I don't have to listen to another word to understand the danger involved. And you realize it too," Sinclair growled.

"Please," Charlie pleaded.

Worth walked toward them. "Charlie. Jasper. I thought you returned to your estate for the rest of the season. What brings you to town?"

"Colebourne and his mad schemes," Sinclair muttered.

"Uncle Theo requested my help, and I promised him I would. But Jasper believes it is too dangerous," Charlie informed Worth.

"It is. Tell her Colebourne's plans are madness. There must be another way to capture Lady Langdale than to risk Charlie's life," Sinclair ranted.

Worth had a sickening suspicion the plan they described was one they kept from him. But why? Was his mother a diversion to keep him away while they conspired together? He turned at the footsteps headed in their direction and saw his mother rushing to interrupt his conversation with the Sinclairs. The guilty expression she wore told him he had guessed right.

"I wish I could tell you, Sinclair, but I've no clue on what everyone has discussed. It appears they kept me out of the loop for some reason. If you will excuse me." He didn't wait for his mother's lies or for Sinclair to respond before opening the door to his brother's study.

Every member of his family filled the study, along with his business partner, Kincaid, and of course Colebourne. Also, shame on him for forgetting the butler too. Everyone but him. They sat spread out near the fireplace in a deep discussion. However, once he entered the study, they grew quiet.

"Interesting how the butler may partake in this discussion, but not I." Worth scoffed. "No offense, Rogers."

Rogers bowed. "None taken, sir."

Worth stalked toward them. "Would someone care to enlighten me to what the discussion might be? One that seems to have angered Sinclair for what you request of his wife."

His gaze traveled over the group, but not a single person stepped forward to state what they discussed. At least they all held guilty expressions, especially Reese. Everyone except Colebourne. The duke narrowed his gaze on Worth, judging if he could accept what they discussed.

"Is this meeting because of Sabrina Lancaster?" Worth waited for a reply, but still none was forthcoming. "A.k.a. Ren, the lass who dresses like a boy, who Dracott befriended in the organization. A.k.a. the dowdy companion that used to be Lady Langdale's right-hand girl. A.k.a. the girl who befriended Evelyn. A.k.a. the girl who I've fallen for."

He paused again, waiting to announce his last bit. They assumed he didn't know. However, he had figured it out before any of them. Well, probably not Colebourne. "Sabrina, otherwise known as Sabrina Langdale, Barbara Langdale's stepdaughter. The baron's daughter he had with Helen Lancaster after they had been married for five years. A blessing to them after the many miscarriages Helen had suffered from. The same girl who disappeared when Lady Langdale snuck away to the Continent. A lost soul who no one cared about enough to save her from a life of hell."

Worth stopped before Colebourne. "I do not know who to express my anger towards. You? Or Dracott and Ravencroft for not rescuing her from the terror she exists in? I am ashamed of your actions."

"As you should be," Colebourne declared.

Ravencroft tried to defend his actions. "We tried, but Sabrina went back to Lady Langdale."

"She is a mere girl," Worth growled.

"She is far from defenseless," Dracott muttered. "I made sure of that."

Worth turned on him. "And now? Are you making sure now when she has to keep returning to her clutches after every order Lady Langdale demands her to follow? When she is forever at the mercy of that diabolical bitch?"

"Graham," Lady Worthington warned.

Worth held up his hand. "Do not reprimand me, Mother, as if I am out of line. We both damn well know I'm not."

Lady Worthington frowned her dislike at his coarse language but didn't reprimand him again. She took a seat on the sofa next to Evelyn.

Worth raked his hands through his hair. "Why?"

"You stated it yourself," Ralston explained. "You have fallen for the girl. Your emotions are too unstable to remain objective, let alone to be aware of the danger surrounding you by your involvement with Sabrina."

"Bull," Worth muttered.

"How did you know of all her disguises and her true identity? No one else had pieced that together," Colebourne asked.

Worth blew out a breath. "Because I have lived and breathed this investigation for close to six years. I have memorized every aspect and learned every player in this game. A few years ago, I discovered the baron shared a child with his first wife. However, every source I contacted didn't remember what happened to her. Every report Falcone turned in never mentioned a young girl. However, the reports mentioned multiple people we could never identify. Those people were Sabrina in disguise."

Dracott shifted. "She learned to be clever in hiding her form after her curves showed and made her uncomfortable. Lady L didn't care to have a gentleman ogling Sabrina when she wanted their attention focused on her. Sabrina was uncomfortable with the extra attention."

Worth looked at Ravencroft. "What did you mean when you said she returned?"

Ravencroft sat forward, and Noel placed her hand on his arm in support. "I found a way for Dracott and I to leave. However, Dracott pleaded with me to help Sabrina too. I didn't want to because I didn't care for how she influenced Dracott. I never understood why my brother was so attached to her. To be honest, I was jealous of their relationship, and because of my envy, I resented and never trusted Sabrina. However, I set my opinion to the side at Dracott's request and helped secure her a place to hide. However, our mother had hidden herself in the same village. Once she saw Sabrina, she turned her over to Lady L to secure her position in the organization."

"And your feelings for Sabrina now?" Worth asked.

Ravencroft squeezed Noel's hand. "After Dracott and Colebourne explained her motives, I deeply regret my ill-treatment toward her."

Worth settled into a chair. "And her motives are?"

Colebourne drummed his fingers on the armchair. "How did you make the connection between all of her disguises?"

Worth tightened his hands into fists with his irritation at Colebourne for avoiding the truth. "A variety of incidents. First, when I chased a pickpocket, I noticed she was a girl. Then Dracott sought his amusement at my expense after he returned the stolen money, as if a thief would just hand over their fleece. Second, Falcone and I followed the dowdy companion into a store. But when I entered, I couldn't find her, and the shopkeeper kept me busy until Sabrina made her escape disguised as a lad. However, the valise she carried sat on the counter. And near the counter sat a display of sequined hair clips that Sabrina had worn with her mermaid costume."

He paused as Evelyn and Eden gasped at his discovery. "When Maggie and Evelyn told Mother the girl's name I had avoided an introduction to and described her costume, all the pieces came together for me."

Worth jumped to his feet, too antsy to stay seated. "You see, I had met the mermaid in the garden that night. After our visit, I wondered who she might be. I spent time with her again last night and followed her home. Once I found their hideout, I dragged Ralston back there. However, we were too late. They vanished as if they had never stayed there."

Ralston shook his head. "You had the wrong house."

"I might agree if I hadn't found one of those hair clips in the bedroom. It was the correct house," Worth argued.

"If they vanished in a rush, it meant they had spotted you trailing them," Dracott explained.

"So you already knew her identity when you inquired about her at the ball last night?" Colebourne demanded.

Worth nodded. "Yes."

Colebourne pointed his cane at the chair. "Sit back down, boy, and I will explain it all."

Worth obeyed Colebourne. If not, the old man would refuse to tell him anything.

"A few years before your brother's involvement with Lady Langdale, there were reports of a rash of robberies at different estates during house parties they held. My brother was a victim of one of these heists. Rumors circulated of who the culprit was since the person attended all these parties," Colebourne started.

Worth interrupted. "Barbara Langdale."

"Yes. But during that time, she went by the name of Barbara Davell. Since some of my family heirlooms were stolen, I called upon Lord Langdale. The baron owed me a few favors for some unfortunate circumstances I had helped him with." Colebourne frowned from the coughs expressed by the various gentlemen around the room. They knew firsthand the favors Colebourne didn't ask but insisted on.

"Anyway, he showed an interest in Miss Davell, and soon they spoke their vows. I came to discover that, right before his death, he only married her to gain information on her crimes. He wrote me a letter, telling me of her crimes but how he still gathered evidence. The baron also requested I care for his daughter in case of his death. However, I never saw the letter until it was too late to help Sabrina." Colebourne wiped at his brow with a handkerchief.

"Since Sabrina was an orphan with no living relatives, Barbara played the martyr and stepped forward and adopted Sabrina, claiming her inheritance for herself. As soon as I realized what happened, I petitioned the courts, but since I had no solid proof of the baron's revelations, they denied my guardianship. No matter what strings I tried to pull, nothing worked. Later, I learned how Barbara had blackmailed the peers who blocked my request for her silence in revealing their sins."

Colebourne cleared his throat. "After Reese and Evelyn married, Barbara declared to whomever would listen how she would seek her revenge one day. Sabrina overheard Barbara bragging about how she had blackmailed Selina Pemberton to do her bidding to ruin Gemma. Sabrina grew suspicious of Barbara's unkind treatment. She never understood why the lady had adopted her. So Sabrina dug through her father's papers he had kept hidden. Before he had died, he swore Sabrina to secrecy about what he discovered."

Rogers poured Colebourne a glass of water. After taking a few sips, Colebourne continued with his story. "Sabrina read through the papers, shocked at what her father documented. She came to me with her father's information, and I tried to persuade her to allow me to help her, but she refused. She wanted to finish her father's work, and over the years, she has stayed in contact with me, relaying information."

Worth shook his head. "You should never have allowed her to stay."

Colebourne sighed. "You are correct. However, each time I made a demand to remove her, the less I heard from her."

"What does she continue to search for?" Worth asked.

Dracott answered. "Lady Langdale has kept journals of every heist and crime she committed in detail. Even down to what she wore. Sabrina has acquired these journals."

"Then what keeps her under Lady L's control?" Worth demanded.

Dracott looked at Colebourne, and the duke nodded for him to tell Worth. "Her search for proof of her father's murder."

"Oh, the poor dear," Lady Worthington cried. "That explains the sadness lingering in her eyes."

Worth looked at his mother in surprise. "You noticed that too?"

"Yes," his mother replied.

Worth nodded and looked away from everyone, gathering his emotions under control. "Does the proof even exist?"

"She believes it does." Colebourne took another drink of water. "When she resurfaced in London this year, I held tremendous relief. I thought I could convince her to leave. Until Sabrina told me of Lady L's latest threat."

Worth pointed at the Sinclairs. "Does this involve Charlie and Sinclair's argument in the hallway?"

"Yes. Sabrina informed me at the ball about an incident planned for Friday," Colebourne said.

"One that involves my wife," Reese said quietly, so Worth understood the seriousness of the threat.

Worth glanced around the study, waiting for more of an explanation. Evelyn took pity on him. "I am to meet Sabrina for tea at a shoppe in Mayfair."

Worth sat forward in his chair. "Sabrina would never hurt you, Evelyn."

Evelyn smiled with sadness at him. "I know she wouldn't, Graham."

"But while she remains within Lady L's clutches, she must follow through with her demands. Ravencroft and I believe Lady Langdale is forcing Sabrina to lure Evelyn into a trap. We've left Lady L desperate enough that she wants to strike out with her anger and hopefully make mistakes along the way. Despite that, we are leery because of how clever she is," Dracott stated.

"And you want Charlie to pretend to be Evelyn," Worth guessed.

"With Evelyn's health, we don't want to risk injury to her or the babe. However, if I pretend to be Evelyn, then I can defend myself better than she could. We are hoping I can convince Sabrina to leave," Charlie explained.

Worth drummed his fingers together while he thought over their plan. "I can understand Sinclair's issue with this plan. It is dangerous and places Charlie at risk. Sabrina will refuse Charlie. What guarantees do we have that Lady L will be near?"

Dracott stood and walked over to the windows. "Because her ego is so inflated, she believes she is invisible."

"That nothing or no one can touch her!" Ravencroft spat.

"She was careless when she arrived to collect Sabrina from the ball and didn't realize you followed her home until her men spotted you watching the house." Dracott tapped at the window. "Even now, she sits across the way and watches us."

Worth leapt to his feet to see, but Dracott stepped in front of him. "Do not give her the satisfaction. Let her believe we are clueless about her activities."

"Then tell me the plan you have contrived to end this terror on Friday," Worth demanded.

"We will fill the shoppe with our people," Ralston explained.

"She knows everyone we are acquainted with," Worth argued.

Kincaid spoke for the first time. "She hasn't seen all of my men or their wives."

"Go on," Worth said.

"We expect Lady L to enter wearing a disguise and make her move on Evelyn. However, she will be unprepared for Charlie. Kincaid's men will have the tea shoppe surrounded inside and out, taking her by surprise. There are some flaws in the plan to work through. But we have faith we can bring about Barbara Langdale's demise on Friday," Ralston said.

"And if we don't. What then?" Worth whispered.

No one uttered a word. What could they say? If it failed, they not only risked Charlie's life but Sabrina's, too. The girl had never held a chance at a simple life, and if they botched this plan, she never would. And Graham wanted to share a simple life with Sabrina with all his heart.

He had admitted how he had fallen for Sabrina, but not how deeply. If he told them how much he loved her, they would've refused to share any of this information with him. He understood their reasoning, but still it bothered him that they thought he would sacrifice everything he worked for because of his feelings for Sabrina.

But wouldn't he?

Chapter Twelve

ONCE THEY FINALIZED THEIR plan, Graham left Reese's study and never looked back. He held a grudge of resentment at them for keeping him away from their discussion. Also, they held no faith in his ability to persevere through a crisis after proving himself worthy of their respect. They still considered him the carefree bachelor who walked through life without a care in the world.

He spent the next hours walking aimlessly, reflecting on what had brought him to this point in his life. Graham found himself at the house he took Sabrina to. He had purchased the house because it was close to his office and where he could escape the craziness of his family when he so desired. He never wanted to sour his experience of relaxation by bringing a lady there. Graham showed Sabrina the house because he thought she would see it as a refuge, too. Also, he hoped she might visit if she ever needed to seek the same comfort.

He let himself in and started a fire. Relaxing in a chair with his feet propped up on a stool, Graham lifted a bottle of whiskey to his lips and took a long swallow. The fiery heat warmed his soul from the chill of listening to Sabrina's tragic story. While he had figured out her various identities, he never knew how she sacrificed herself to bring her father's murderer to justice. Still, she suffered more than Dracott and Ravencroft even realized.

The crackling fire lured him to sleep. It wasn't long before his nightmare returned to haunt his sleep. However, something pulled at him to awaken before his chase for Sabrina began. He dragged his eyes open to see a vision of Sabrina before him. Graham shook his head and tried to refocus, thinking he might still be asleep. He sat forward and took another drink.

But when his eyes adjusted to the darkness, Sabrina was sitting on the sofa with her legs pulled in front of her and her arms wrapped around them. Her feet were bare, and she wore a thin nightgown. Sorrow flowed from her gaze, wrapping Graham in her torment. His nightmare played out before him. Her behavior reflected how she acted in his dreams.

Graham stumbled to her side, sat next to her, and held out his hand toward her. He hesitated to touch her, afraid she was only a figment of his imagination. He pressed his hand forward, resting it over her clasped fingers, and then pulled them back quickly. She wasn't part of his nightmare, but a dream come true.

"You are real," Graham whispered. "I thought I had imagined you."

Sabrina laid her head on her knees, facing him. "Perhaps you are."

Graham stroked his hand through her hair that surrounded her like a curtain. The soft strands gave him more proof of her existence. "No, I am not."

Graham settled back against the cushions, his hand still entangled in her hair. He never asked her the question of what brought her to him because he didn't wish to break the spell holding them captive. She'd tell him if she wanted to.

"Why are you drinking?" Sabrina asked.

Graham frowned. "I suppose I had hoped the whiskey would ease my troubles."

Sabrina searched his gaze for what troubled him. "I do not like when you frown. It makes me want to make you smile."

Sabrina's comment confused Graham. He didn't recall frowning while in her presence, because he had no reason to. Every moment they spent together, his smile spread wide. She brought him such joy. That only meant, while he searched for her everywhere, she had watched him from afar.

Graham bent his head close to hers and pressed his lips against hers softly. "I have no reason to frown when you are near."

Sabrina traced a finger across his lips. "Then why are you not smiling now?"

Graham wrapped his hand around Sabrina's neck to keep her close. "Because the feelings I hold are more powerful than what a smile can express."

Sabrina stared into Graham's eyes. The message of his desire for her poured out from the depths of his gaze. When she ran here to escape from her thoughts, she didn't think she would find Graham. It was wrong of her to invite herself into his house without his permission. But her need to be near him drew her inside his home.

She expected him to question her attire and lack of shoes, but he never asked a single question as to why she was there. After he reassured himself she wasn't a figment of his imagination, she offered him the comfort he needed. In return, he gifted her with the same comfort she never asked from him. How did they accept each other with such ease? Were they each other's destiny and neither of them thought to question otherwise? Sabrina didn't know if she believed in fate, but the way Graham treated her made her ask the loaded question: was he her soul mate?

Sabrina stood and held out her hand to Graham. He rose, sliding his fingers between hers, and followed Sabrina as she climbed the stairs. She held no clue where his bedchamber was but allowed fate to guide her. It guided her to a plain bedchamber containing a wardrobe, a bathtub, and a bed. The curtains were spread wide, allowing the moon to light the bedchamber brighter than a candle would.

Sabrina turned and stood on her tiptoes to brush her lips across Graham's mouth. Her need for Graham's love took over the kiss, and she expressed her desires with every desperate pull of her lips against his. Her hands cupped his cheeks. The soft bristles showed Sabrina how Graham's refusal to shave was because he loved her hands caressing him.

It wasn't the effects of the whiskey that slowed Graham from pulling Sabrina into his arms and claiming possession over their kisses. Her desperate affection toward him pulled his emotions in more impossible directions, and he was incapable of expressing himself. He ached to strip the gown from her body, lay her on his bed, and make love to her. He wanted to show Sabrina the special place she held in his heart with each kiss and caress, a place he had never allowed another soul to claim. Graham held back because he needed Sabrina to accept he was her fate. Her destiny. She was created for him alone.

Graham set his hands on her waist, urging her closer. At his touch, she sighed into their kiss, relaxing against him. What Graham hadn't realized before was how much his touch calmed her. While he held himself back, he gave Sabrina doubt on how much he wanted her. With each gentle touch drawing their bodies but a breath apart, Sabrina's kisses turned into a desperate need of showing Graham how she stood before him with her heart open to the possibility of their love.

Sabrina pulled back from Graham and took a few steps backwards. She stared into his eyes, and what she saw amazed her. She never expected to see his love for her shining brightly. Sabrina had thought she caught his fancy, but she never imagined he loved her as she did him. While he never expressed the words, she knew he would one day.

But not while Sabrina kept her secrets from him.

She didn't want to keep them, but she knew no other way. Nor did she want to hurt him with her deceit. Or cause his family to doubt his intentions regarding her. Graham was an honorable gentleman, and while he spent time with her, he violated every ethic he held himself accountable to. However, her desperate need for Graham's love made her too selfish to turn her back on him and walk out of his life.

Graham watched every doubt and indecision cross her features. Sabrina stared intently into his eyes. Did she see his love reflected? He believed she did, but she never expressed if she felt the same. However, he didn't think she needed to hear the words either. Every soft kiss and gentle caress showed what they feared to admit.

He pulled his shirt from his trousers and went to work on the buttons. After he undid a few, he pulled his shirt over his head and dropped it to the floor. Sabrina reached out and slid her hand across his chest. Graham moaned at how her touch affected him. Sabrina's teeth scraped across her bottom lip as her hand dipped lower to rest across the placket of his trousers. When her gaze raised to his, asking for his permission, he nodded, biting back his groan.

Her fingers trembled as she undid each button. Sabrina slid to her knees when she finished and urged them over his hips and down his legs. After he stepped out of them, she slowly rose, trailing her hands along the front of his legs. The slight touch of her palm grazed against his cock before she stepped away from him again.

"Sabrina," he growled, unable to hold back how she affected him.

An impish grin lit her face, catching him by surprise. She twirled away from him and undid the ribbon holding her nightgown together. With one pull, the gown opened, teasing Graham. But Sabrina didn't keep him waiting long to view her splendid body. She slid the gown off her shoulders, and it pooled at her feet.

Then she wrapped her arm around the bed column above her head and leaned back, waiting for him to come to her. When he stood spellbound at her siren's pose, she lifted her other hand at him and bent her finger, beckoning him to her side.

"Graham," Sabrina whispered to tempt him closer.

After years of dressing as a boy or the ugly companion to her stepmother, Sabrina had convinced herself she was a plain girl who would never entice a gentleman to look twice at her. However, at this moment, Graham made her feel beautiful beyond words with the stare he directed at her. If he didn't pull her into his arms soon, Sabrina thought she would melt at his feet.

Sabrina giggled at the image. Her eyes grew wide, and she covered her mouth, shocked she had let the giggle slip out. Graham cocked his eyebrow at her display of amusement and narrowed his gaze. He stalked toward her one slow step at a time, drawing out his reaction to her giggle.

His hands slid up and down her arms before grabbing her hips and pulling their bodies together. Her soft curves fit perfectly against his hardened muscles. Sabrina gasped at the intimate contact.

"Is there something you find amusing, my siren?" Graham whispered in her ear before licking a path along her neck.

Sabrina threw her head back against the column, arching her neck at his attack on her senses. She had forgotten her slight amusement with each lick and nip. However, Graham meant to torment her until he heard an answer to his question.

Graham raised Sabrina's leg around his hip and pressed his cock into her heated core. The warmth beckoned him to slide inside her and allow her wetness to ease the ache consuming him. When he rotated his hips against her, Sabrina's fingers dug into his arm. No longer a giggle escaped her lips, but her moan of desire rang through the air instead.

"What, no more giggles? Only moans?" Graham dipped his head to slide a nipple between his lips.

He glanced up as he teased her with a soft bite. Her impish delight no longer graced her face. Instead, she pulled her lips into a seductive smile, tempting him to discover every facet of her desires.

Sabrina never imagined two people could find humor in the act of sex. But what she shared with Graham was more than a sexual act between two people only wishing to reach gratification. What they shared was their two hearts accepting every nuisance of the person they were with.

Sabrina smirked. "Perhaps my giggles are part of my siren's call to lure you closer. It appeared it worked quite well."

"Is that so?" Graham slid a finger along her wet folds. "For a minute, my pirate's ego suffered from your amusement."

"Yes, well, it appears your ego has made a remarkable recovery." Sabrina gasped as Graham slid another finger inside her.

"Oh, I am not so sure," Graham mused, watching Sabrina's eyes darken with desire. "But after I claim my bounty, we shall see if I recover."

Sabrina moaned. "If not?"

"Then I guess I shall have to keep claiming my bounty until I do," Graham promised.

Graham's declaration stated what he wanted from Sabrina. Her complete surrender. And she was more than willing to succumb to his every demand as long as he never stopped his exquisite claiming of her soul.

Sabrina whimpered when Graham slid her leg back down and pulled her hand off him. He slid her arm up the bed column and held her two hands together. "Keep still, my love. Or else I shall tie you up with my pirate's rope." Graham winked at her and knelt before her.

Sabrina's lashes fluttered as she watched Graham raise her leg back up again and throw it over his shoulder. He looked up to see if she obeyed his command, then struck his tongue against her folds with a bold stroke, making her tremble around him.

Graham pulled back in pleasure at her response, licking his lips. She tasted more refreshing than the whiskey he sought to escape his problems with. He didn't need whiskey to chase away his demons; he only needed Sabrina. His gaze raked her body from her arms entwined around the column to the desire flaring from her eyes and along her chest to where her back arched from the pleasure of his tongue. Her breasts rose and fell with each quickened breath she drew. Her rosy nipples pebbled into hardened buds. His gaze dipped to her flat stomach that flared out across her hips that he held onto as his mouth devoured her sweet core.

He turned his head and pressed a kiss into her thigh to calm her trembling, then returned to her wet folds and savored her sweet flavor on his tongue. He pressed his face in and slid his tongue inside her, his mouth open to enjoy her succulent nectar.

Sabrina moaned. "Graham."

The bristles on his cheeks scraped across the sensitive skin of her thighs, sending delicious tingles coursing through her. She wanted to reach down and run her fingers through his hair and hold his head to her core, but she didn't dare disobey his command. Even though he made it in jest, Sabrina loved the game they played and wanted the sweet torture to continue. Instead, she rocked her hips in rhythm with the delicious dance of his tongue. When his fingers dug into her hips, she knew he found as much pleasure in the gift he gave her as she did in receiving the pleasures he stirred in her soul.

Graham drew in a deep breath, inhaling Sabrina's essence into his soul. She might've obeyed his command to keep her hands still, but that didn't stop the rest of her body from responding. When she rocked her hips against his mouth, making her own command, he knew he wouldn't last much longer. His need to make them one dominated his senses.

With one last slide of his tongue, he slid up her body. "Sabrina," Graham growled.

"Mmm," Sabrina murmured, lost in the ecstasy he surrounded them in.

"Wrap your arms around my shoulders and hold on," Graham demanded.

"Is that another pirate command?" Her teasing whisper washed across his senses, earning her another growl.

"No, 'tis a plea from a man who wishes to slide inside your sweet warmth and lose himself in your wet canal to help ease his desperate need to become one with you." Graham lifted her legs up to wrap around his waist and pressed his cock against her wet core.

"Oh." Sabrina gasped as his smooth cock settled against her. The heavy weight pulsed with desire between them.

She slid her arms off the column and wrapped them around his shoulders, pressing her breasts against his muscled chest.

Her nipples tightened at the contact of his warmth, sending a rush of desire to her core. As she clung to him, Graham lifted her body higher and eased her slowly onto his cock. His fullness spread her apart.

"I'm sorry, love. It might hurt a bit, but do not let go," Graham whispered in Sabrina's ear, fighting back the urge to lower her and pierce her in one swift move.

Sabrina never tensed once. She had heard of the pain suffered from the first time, but Graham's tender care kept her relaxed. She was ready to endure the brief discomfort for the precious moments of passion that sought its release and held them spellbound.

Sabrina couldn't help herself. She didn't want Graham to regret hurting her. "I thought a pirate found victory with his every plunder."

Graham pressed his forehead against Sabrina's and closed his eyes, fighting the urge to slide deep inside her and laughing at her jest. He opened his eyes to stare into her mischief-filled eyes that also held the same need he clung to. His kiss turned rough from the emotions she stirred in his soul. "God, I love you."

His kiss gentled after his declaration. He had never meant to express his love until they held no secrets between them. But his love of her innocence, silliness, and passion forever held him at her mercy, and he could no longer stay quiet.

Graham slowly eased Sabrina down onto his cock, pushing past her resistance. He captured her gasp at the invasion and increased the pressure of his kiss the deeper she sank around him. Sabrina dug her fingers into his shoulders and returned his hungry kisses with her own.

Graham's endearment shook Sabrina's very foundation. The emotions he expressed with those simple words flooded Sabrina's senses with so much hope. She didn't even realize the tears sliding down her cheeks until they mingled with their kiss.

Graham rocked, urging Sabrina's body up and down. Her nipples scraped against his chest with each motion. Her wet core guided his cock in and out of her in a smooth caress. Each time he drew her down on him deeper, her pussy tightened, gripping him with her desire.

The salt of her tears lingered on his tongue, and he paused, ready to withdraw, waiting for her plea. But it never came, only the soft moans of pleasure he drew from her each time he entered her and rocked his hips against hers. He pressed up into Sabrina harder and deeper.

"Graham!" Sabrina's moan echoed around them. She arched her body at his invasion. "More," she demanded.

Sabrina swayed against Graham, easing the ache consuming her. She felt herself drowning in their passion. However, Graham's powerful hold kept her anchored to him. Graham followed her command and slid in and out of her with such force Sabrina lost herself to the pleasure.

Graham buried his head in Sabrina's neck, sucking on her flesh as he plundered her, taking his pleasure with each stroke. They were both slipping over the edge together. Her pussy gripped his throbbing cock. Their bodies made their demands of their need to surrender to the passion and accept its fate.

"Sabrina," Graham roared as he sent them over the edge and into the paradise of floating as one.

Sabrina's body shook all around them. Graham walked them toward the bed and slid her body down the length of him. He tipped her head back and devoured her lips, showing Sabrina he was far from finished with her. He picked her up and tossed her onto the bed. Graham didn't want to give her a moment to ponder his declaration. He would leave her in no doubt about how much she meant to him. No amount of lies or secrets changed how much he loved her.

Sabrina laughed at how Graham threw her on the bed. But when she saw the determination and desire in his eyes, she slowly slid back, unsure of his intentions. Or if her emotions could handle another onslaught of the passion he stirred inside her.

"Graham, what are you about?" Sabrina scooted back across the bed.

Graham placed his knee on the bed as he climbed on top of it. His hands wrapped around Sabrina's ankles and drew her back to him. "It seems my ego still suffers, so I must claim my bounty again."

"Oh my!" Sabrina exclaimed when Graham pulled her underneath him.

His mouth wrapped around her nipples, sucking greedily, while his fingers slid between her folds and stroked her desires back to life again. It would appear her pirate's ego suffered a tragic blow, and she must endure his ravishing long into the night.

God, she loved him too.

Chapter Thirteen

A FEW HOURS LATER, Sabrina slipped out of Graham's bed and pulled her nightgown back on. She stole a glance at him after tying the ribbon. She had stayed longer than she should've and must leave. But she hadn't been able to resist Graham. He stirred to life their passion with every kiss and caress, entrancing her to become his willing captive.

Graham lay on his stomach, sprawled across the bed with his head resting on the pillow and his arms thrown off to the side. Sabrina crawled onto the bed and sat with her legs folded underneath her. She bent over and pressed a kiss across his cheek. Since she couldn't help herself, she also fluttered her fingers through his thick hair. With a sigh, she disentangled herself and left Graham. Sabrina was a coward who wanted to avoid what his gaze would hold.

She had risked enough by visiting him and would suffer for it once she returned. If not by bruises, then by Lady L's revenge on someone Sabrina cared for. Her stepmother had discovered other ways to torment her when Sabrina learned not to cry in pain from the brutal treatment of the guards. Dracott had taken the brunt of Sabrina's punishment and never once held it against her. He had even comforted her, drying her tears after his beatings. With Dracott gone, Lady L would find another victim to inflict her fury on.

Sabrina slipped on her shoes and drew her coat around her. When she broke into his home, she hadn't expected to find him there. But as she sat on the sofa watching him sleep, she had noticed the stress settled around his eyes and how tightly he clutched the bottle of whiskey. She wasn't a fool not to understand how she caused his problems.

When he woke up and mumbled she was only part of his dream, something had shifted in Sabrina. She had realized how much she cared for him. Sabrina had feared that, if she didn't steal this piece of time with him, she would never get another chance to treasure his warm embrace.

She returned to the sofa, picked up the bottle of whiskey, and set it back where it belonged. Sabrina had the desire to savor a sip. She had witnessed her own father's decline when he escaped his problems with the promise the spirits held. However, she had no wish to follow the same path. Sabrina must remain steadfast for the days to come.

Graham's suit coat had fallen to the floor, and she picked it up to lie across the arm of the chair. The light from the fire flickered, casting a glow around an object. Sabrina bent over to retrieve it. It wasn't one but two of her sequined hair clips. She had only left one for him as a clue. Where did he get the other one? Did he purchase it from the Fitzgeralds' store when he followed her in there? He must have.

Sabrina glanced toward the stairs, remembering Graham's desperation as they made love. His urging to trust him rang clear. He knew the truth about Sabrina Lancaster. Every sordid detail.

And he still loved her.

Sabrina ran. There was no need for her to run, other than her need to escape the truth. But it was pointless. It didn't alter how Graham felt about her one bit. Nor did it change how she felt about him. After all, one couldn't change what fate had set out for them. They must accept it as their destiny.

Sabrina slowed down, catching her breath. In her haste to leave Graham's house, she didn't pay attention to her surroundings. Her gaze scanned the horizon, and she tensed when she saw a figure striding toward her. But the closer the person drew, the more relief settled over Sabrina. Instead of waiting for the lecture that would fall upon her ears, she started walking again. However, she kept her steps slow so her friend could catch up with her.

"You can at least stop. You owe me that much at least," Dracott demanded, reaching out to grab her arm.

His hold reminded her of the occurrences when he had saved her from trouble. She slowed to a stop. Sabrina owed Dracott a lot more than his simple request. She owed him her loyalty, at the very least, for how he had protected her from herself.

"Follow me before they come around the corner." Dracott led her over to a building. He dug in his pocket for the key and unlocked the door, ushering her inside before easing the door closed.

Sabrina followed him into the office. So lost in her thoughts, she hadn't realized how close she was to Graham's office. She walked over to his desk and curled up in his chair while Dracott peeked through the window shutters to see if anyone followed them. She ran her hands across the desktop, wanting to share a connection with Graham. Sabrina had watched him from across the street as he sat at the desk, working or talking with his partner.

Dracott dragged a chair next to her and sat down. "What are you doing, Ren?"

Sabrina shrugged. "It appears I am talking to you and avoiding the hired thugs."

Dracott frowned, not appreciating her attempt at humor. "With Worth."

Sabrina stared at him with a forlorn expression. "Is it so wrong to capture a few joyous memories for myself?"

Dracott glanced away for a second before glancing back at Sabrina. "Yes, and no."

Sabrina's lips pinched together as she fought back tears. She couldn't talk without falling apart. She hadn't felt more lost than she did now. The very person she had always depended on questioned her motives.

Dracott gathered Sabrina's hands in his. "You are allowed every joyous memory you can capture. I question what this is between you and Worth because I care for both of you. I don't wish to see either of you hurt. And while you continue to stay under Lady L's thumb, you risk both his and your life."

"I am close," Sabrina promised.

"You have said that for years. Yet every lead you have falls through. It is time to leave and welcome the life you've always dreamed of," Dracott urged.

Sabrina withdrew her hands. "I cannot."

Dracott leaned back in his chair and dragged his hand down his face. "Explain to me why. Help me understand your reason. Perhaps I can help."

Sabrina shook her head. "No. You've gotten away and started a life with Maggie. I will not put you at risk."

"But you will risk Worth's life?" Dracott taunted.

Sabrina ran her hands over the arms of Graham's chair. "I do not mean to," she whispered.

"She will hurt him to destroy you," Dracott warned.

"I know!" Sabrina cried. "Do you think I'm not aware of what she will do?"

"She will torment him worse than any way she tormented me. Because she can see how much you love him. Hell! I see how much you care for him."

Sabrina tore out of the chair and paced away from Dracott. "Then I will stay away from him from here on out. I will disappear, and he will never find me. Is that what you wish for me to promise?"

Dracott moved to Sabrina and drew her into his arms. "No. I want you to come home with me so we can guarantee your safety. Please, Sabrina. End this madness tonight."

Sabrina could no longer hold back her tears. Each drop held sorrow, regret, the promises she never kept, and the heartache she carried with her wherever she went. She collapsed in Dracott's arms from the burdens she had carried for so long, unable to live with them anymore.

Dracott lifted Sabrina in his arms, carried her to the sofa, and sat down, comforting her as he used to in the past. She wasn't only his best friend; she was the sister he never had. He rested his chin on her head and waited for her to get herself under control.

"He knows who I am, doesn't he?" Sabrina whispered.

"Yes."

Sabrina sighed. "I thought he might."

Dracott tipped her chin up. He wanted to see her reaction when he asked his question. "What does she have planned for Evelyn on Friday?"

Another wave of tears fell at his question. "She wants to kill her."

Dracott drew in a deep breath. "They will hold you as an accomplice and you will hang."

"No!"

"Yes!" Dracott emphasized with force.

"I warned Colebourne," Sabrina explained.

Dracott tried to get through to her. "The authorities will not care about your meager warning. They will only care how someone killed a peer and you did nothing to prevent the crime."

Sabrina untangled herself from Dracott's lap. "I must leave."

Dracott blew out a breath. Sabrina was as stubborn as ever. He thought he might convince her to leave, but she wouldn't be swayed. Obviously, a night spent in Worth's arms wasn't enough to change her mind, either. Their only hope was for Sabrina to come to her senses and break the hold Lady Langdale kept her under. She must stop protecting every other victim and start protecting herself instead.

"At least let me walk you to where you need to turn off," Dracott offered.

Sabrina nodded. She waited for Dracott to lock the office, and they started down the alleyway. Neither one of them said anything. Everything that needed to be said had been. Now they walked alongside each other, each wishing for understanding of the dire circumstances that prevented them from surrendering their point of view.

Sabrina wished more than anyone to leave, but to do so, she would have to admit defeat and accept she would never vindicate her father's death. To walk away also meant Lady L would never be held accountable for her crimes. The woman had caused nothing but destruction to so many innocent victims. All because she held immense pleasure in destroying a soul to display her power. She was the perfect example of a villain, and Sabrina hated villains with a passion.

Sabrina stopped. "We must part once again, my friend."

Dracott pleaded one last time. "Will you please reconsider?"

"What is it you wish for Sabrina to reconsider?" Lady Langdale stepped out of the shadows, her two guards flanking her sides.

Sabrina stepped in front of Dracott, opening her arms wide. "Nothing."

Dracott had never allowed Sabrina to protect him from Lady Langdale, and he wouldn't start now. "To return home with me."

An unsettling laugh rang from Lady Langdale. "Is your wife open to sharing her marriage bed with Sabrina? I do not suppose Lady Margaret's brother would care for the sleeping arrangements. Would he, Sabrina? Especially since you spread your legs for him this evening and he tasted your charms. Graham Worthington seems like the jealous type."

Dracott curled his hands into fists. "Still as crude as ever, I see."

Lady L made an irritating tsking noise. "Ah, but, Dracott, we are cut from the same cloth. Do not think since you've married a peer of the ton, they consider you anything more than how you were born. A bastard."

Dracott didn't respond to Lady Langdale. He wasn't in the mood for her mind games after sitting outside of Worth's home, waiting for Sabrina to leave, then the heart-wrenching conversation he shared with her. He had never seen Sabrina break down in such torturous despair. Her agony left him more concerned for her than ever.

"Ah, boys." Lady L smirked at her guards. "Dracott is not arguing, which only means he knows how correct I am. However, as much as we may agree, it does not alter how furious I am with Sabrina for leading him so close to our new residence." Lady L circled Dracott and Sabrina. "You remember how Sabrina used to have to meet her punishment, don't you, Dracott?"

"No!" Sabrina screamed. "Do not lay a hand on him."

"Sabrina," Dracott warned.

Sabrina refused to allow him to take her punishment anymore. She was the one at fault, and she would suffer the consequences of her mistakes. "Run," she ordered Dracott.

Dracott refused. "No."

Lady L snapped her fingers, and two more guards came out of the darkness. One of them yanked Sabrina away from Dracott and pinned her arms behind her back, while the other three circled Dracott, taunting him by shoving him back and forth amongst themselves.

"Stop," Sabrina cried, fighting against her captor's hold.

Her screams amused the brutes, and they started their torment, punching Dracott in the ribs and across the face, sending him sprawling to the ground. With his every attempt to rise, they knocked him down again. His beating was more brutal than Sabrina had ever witnessed before. But Dracott never faltered. He kept defending himself to the best of his ability. Sabrina's cries grew louder, her hoarse voice bellowing out her demands while tears streamed down her face.

"Shut her up," Lady L roared.

Sabrina didn't expect the guard to twist her arms tighter and kick the backs of her knees. Sabrina fell to the ground, and the brute kicked her in the side. She let out a piercing scream at the pain ricocheting through her body. But her attacker was far from finished. He lifted her up like she was a rag doll and slugged her across the face. Drops of blood coated her tongue from where her lip split open.

Sabrina held no clue what happened after that. She collapsed to the ground again. Her only recollection was of someone carrying her over their shoulder. Her body jostled with each step, and her face slammed into their muscled back. Pain spread through every part of her body. The only comfort afforded her was when she passed out.

Before her body surrendered to the darkness, she saw Dracott lying on the ground. He never moved once. She prayed he lived.

If not, then his death was on her hands.

Chapter Fourteen

WORTH STRETCHED HIS ARM out, searching the bed for Sabrina. It didn't surprise him when he encountered emptiness. He never meant to fall asleep on her. Even when he closed his eyes as sleep overcame him, he had known she'd disappear before he awoke. His wish for her to stay went ignored, never to be granted.

He rolled over and stared up at the canopy. Then his gaze drifted to the columns holding the canopy up. A wicked smile spread across his face as he remembered how he made Sabrina tremble against the wooden structure. He had brought her body to more trembling heights throughout the evening. Each kiss and caress had been more memorable than the last.

Worth hopped out of bed, ready to begin his day. He didn't have a clue where to start, but he must find Sabrina and show her how he trusted and loved her more than life itself. If he wasn't honest with her, then he couldn't expect her honesty in return.

Worth went to the wardrobe and threw on his scruffiest clothes. He wanted to blend in with the crowd as he searched for Sabrina. He didn't think she would frequent Mayfair again, especially after what he had learned. No. She would frequent the area near the docks. Worth grabbed a hat to pull low on his head to help with his disguise.

When he started down the stairs, he heard movement below, giving him hope Sabrina hadn't left. She had waited for him. Worth rushed down, but she wasn't lingering about.

"Sabrina?" Worth called out.

Silence.

Then a moan echoed from the kitchen. He rushed in, afraid Sabrina had injured herself. Instead, he found Dracott covered in blood, lying on the floor just inside the door.

"Dracott, what in the hell happened?" Worth pulled Dracott to his feet and helped him to the sofa.

Worth ran back to the kitchen and shut the door. He gathered a towel, poured some water into a bowl, and carried them back to the small parlor. Dracott had stretched out, with one arm held against his ribs and his other arm dangling off the sofa.

He winced as he cleared the blood off Dracott's wounds. An unease clung to him at how Dracott's beating revolved around Sabrina.

"Sabrina?"

Dracott peered at Worth with one eye half-open, the other too swollen to lift the lid. He nodded and pointed at the bottle of whiskey sitting on the shelf. Worth glanced around, noticing how Sabrina had straightened his home before she left. His hands shook as he poured Dracott a shot. As much as he would regret not pouring himself one, Worth resisted the spirits. He handed the glass over to Dracott.

Dracott pulled himself to a sitting position, grimacing at the ache coursing through his body. He needed this drink and another one after he told Worth the horrid details of his attack. Once Worth learned of the treatment Sabrina had suffered at the hands of Lady L's guard, he didn't know how he would calm the man. Dracott threw the shot back and signaled for another one. Once Worth filled the glass, Dracott took a few more sips. The whiskey stung the cut on his lip, but it gave him the courage to face Worth.

He leaned back and sighed. "They took her with them. But not before Lady L's guard beat Sabrina severe enough that she passed out. The bitch never stopped him once, only cackled her amusement. She has become unhinged. I fear for Sabrina's life. Usually, the lady pacified herself by issuing Sabrina's punishment onto others. Except this time she made Sabrina suffer too."

"How badly did they beat her?" Worth paced back and forth. His emotions unraveled to a point where he was helpless when the grief consumed him. Without knowing her whereabouts, he couldn't rescue her from the terror she resided in.

"Bad enough to knock her out." Dracott cringed when Worth picked up a chair and threw it across the room. He had expected this rage but didn't realize how it would tear Worth apart. Worth cared for Sabrina more than he imagined.

"Damn!" Worth pulled at his hair. "Why did I fall asleep? I sensed she would flee and yet I left her vulnerable to that bitch."

Dracott took another gulp of the fiery liquid. "You cannot blame yourself. I followed her here and waited for her to leave. I even took her to the office and tried to reason with her. But she refused to leave Lady Langdalc. She wants to seek her vengeance, and nothing I could say made her change her mind. I walked her close enough to their hideout that Sabrina would allow me. However, Lady L and her guards sat waiting to pounce on us. We never stood a chance."

"What do you mean, others suffer from Sabrina's punishment?" Worth asked.

"She used to have her guards punish Sabrina. However, Sabrina refused to cry or show she was in pain. This infuriated Lady Langdale, so she started hurting the people Sabrina cared about," Dracott explained.

"You."

Dracott rubbed at his side. "Yes. While I lived with them, I suffered from the beatings more times than I can count. I would've done anything to protect Sabrina. But if it wasn't me, it would be someone Sabrina had befriended. The less fortunate who Lady L bullied."

"How will we find her?" Worth muttered.

"We need to talk with Rogers. It is time to call in reinforcements."

"Rogers? Reinforcement?" Worth asked.

"Rogers is part of a network of individuals who have connections in the underworld. While they are as dishonest as Lady L, some more so than her, they have no qualms about turning on the others. To our fortune, Lady L has double-crossed most of these people. The last Rogers heard, most of them aspire to end her reign of terror by snuffing out her life." Dracott swung his legs off the sofa.

Worth scoffed. "What, they have standards on evilness?"

Dracott laughed, then groaned in agony. "Of course."

"Can they guarantee Sabrina's safety?"

Dracott looked at Worth with pity. "Nobody can guarantee anything. Also, we must pay a price if they agree to help us."

"Anything," Worth swore.

Dracott struggled to his feet. Once he found his balance, he stared at Worth with a serious expression. "I only have one question to ask. Is she worth sacrificing your beliefs for?"

"I love her."

Just as Dracott thought, but he'd needed Worth to declare the sentiment. "Then let's end this."

A few hours later, Rogers led Worth and Dracott down a flight of stairs to an underground club where every degenerate soul in London came to seek their vice. They had agreed with the others to allow only the three of them to plead their case. Rogers had explained how they sneered upon the upper crust peers, and since Worth held no title and Dracott had spent most of his life in this setting, they might be able to strike a deal.

All his years of striving for an honorable existence had led him to this path. Conspiring with one devil to end the life of another. Worth hadn't realized so many devils roamed the world, each of them fighting to be the one to carry the pitchfork and lure everyone to their own dungeon of hell.

Rogers stopped outside the door in the darkened hallway. "Are you sure about this, sir?"

Worth nodded. "We have no other alternative."

"Very well." He rapped on the door three times, paused, and then rapped off two more knocks.

The door opened without a sound, and Rogers stepped through. Then the door closed, leaving Worth and Dracott outside the room. Rogers had explained how their visit would proceed.

Worth settled against the paneled wall while they waited. "Are you sure you don't want to wait outside in the carriage?"

"No. I am here to follow this through to the end with you. I carry just as much guilt as you do. Please do not cut me off," Dracott answered.

Worth placed his hand on Dracott's shoulder so as not to cause him any more pain. "We will see this through together and bring Sabrina home where she belongs."

Dracott leaned against the wall, while Worth tapped his foot in impatience. Things were progressing too slowly for him. His agonized thoughts over Sabrina's safety and her injuries consumed him. After Maggie cried over Dracott's injuries and Rogers saw to his wounds, they had discussed their next plan of action with everyone. He thought his sister would rant at him and refuse to let Dracott help him find Sabrina, but she had surprised him by wrapping Worth in a hug, swearing they would help him any way they could. His family had expressed their sorrow over the news of Sabrina.

The door opened suddenly, and a guard waved them in. Worth and Dracott walked in slowly, not knowing what to expect. Rogers sat in a chair facing a desk. Behind the desk sat a gentleman around Worth's age, smoking a cigar. The man filled out the chair, not from flab but from muscles that strained against his clothing. His clothing held an immaculate appeal with a black vest over a white shirt and a cravat stiffly pressed against his neck. Worth had expected a degenerate soul, not one with the manners of a gentleman.

"Please take a seat, gentleman." He indicated the two chairs next to Rogers. "We have much to discuss."

Worth and Dracott sat down. "Thank you for agreeing to see us," Worth said.

The gentleman nodded. "I believe we have the same issue that needs dealing with. And it is past the time for us to do so."

"Yes. I agree, Mr. . . ." Worth hesitated. He was unsure how to address the man.

"DeVille."

"Mr. DeVille, we must—"

"No, just DeVille," he interrupted Worth

The man stood and poured himself a drink. He held the bottle out in a silent question if any of them wanted a drink, but they all declined. "Rogers has informed me of Lady L's activities early this morning. It is distressing to learn how she has hurt Sabrina as she has. I do not take kindly to a woman's abuse."

Worth sat on the edge of the chair. "You know Sabrina?"

DeVille held a confident smile that set Worth on edge. "Yes."

"How?" Worth bit out.

DeVille laughed. "Let's just say she is a friend I greatly admire."

Worth fought back the urge to demand what their connection was. Now wasn't the time or place to demonstrate how jealous he was of Sabrina's relationship with this man. Especially if DeVille could help him rescue Sabrina. "What do you suggest we do?"

DeVille peered at Worth, judging if he could trust him. "I made a few inquiries after Rogers made contact. While Sabrina is in a great deal of pain from her injuries, she can move around. I have placed an informant in Lady L's camp, and she is making sure Sabrina gets the care she needs without Lady L's knowledge."

"How?" Worth asked.

DeVille laughed. "How is not important for you to know, Mr. Worthington. The only issue you need to focus on is the details of how we are to bring about Lady L's demise."

Worth gripped the arms of the chair, fighting against his lack of control of the situation. "And that is?"

"Rogers informed mc of your plan for Friday. You will continue with this plan. However, now my people will also be amongst your crowd, and securing Lady L's escape is impossible. She will meet her untimely death, and everyone who is associated with her will meet theirs too. None of your people will have to spill any blood. Once we secure Sabrina and your sister-in-law's safety and lay our trap, your organization can step back and allow us to finish Barbara Langdale," DeVille explained.

"And we are to ignore how we will never seek justice for all those she victimized?" Worth inquired.

DeVille shrugged. "Will her death not be justice enough? I am sure many of those victims would agree."

"And all the years we spent gathering evidence against her?" Worth continued.

DeVille sighed. "Mr. Worthington, you cannot have both. Either Lady L's death or Sabrina's? Because that is Lady L's plan for Friday. Her ultimate plan is to kill Sabrina. Barbara is aware of how Sabrina has found her journals and has proof of her father's murder. Friday is her revenge against Sabrina's betrayal and she uses your family to guilt Sabrina into following her orders. Make your decision."

"Kill her," Worth venomously ordered.

Deville nodded. Rogers stood, indicating their meeting had concluded.

Worth followed Dracott and Rogers to the door, then turned. "And what payment do you demand?"

DeVille took a sip of his drink. "There will come a time when I request a favor in return. This favor will require for you to put aside your beliefs. Is this acceptable to you?"

"If Sabrina survives their ordeal, it is. If she doesn't, we can renegotiate the terms later," Worth stated.

DeVille nodded. "Fair enough, Mr. Worthington."

Worth left the underground club filled with regret for trading part of his soul away to a devil. Yet he also felt a sense of relief that this nightmare would soon end. Once he held Sabrina in his arms again, everything he sacrificed would be worth it.

But would he get the chance again?

Or was Sabrina lost to him forever?

Chapter Fifteen

G RAHAM PULLED THE BRIM of his hat lower as he walked
along the storefronts. He tried to blend in with the
crowd, but he failed miserably. He had searched for Sabrina
at every location they had ever crossed paths with her many
disguises, but he hadn't seen her anywhere. After his meeting
with DeVille, Graham had refused to sit around and wait for
Friday's event to unfold. He must find her. It tore him apart
at how she suffered and he couldn't offer her any comfort or
protection.

There was one last place to try. The bell rang over the door,
announcing his arrival in the Fitzgeralds' shop. Unlike the
disarray in the shop, Mrs. Fitzgerald bustled toward him.

"Ah, you have returned. Are you wanting more of those hair
clips?" Mrs. Fitzgerald teased.

Graham smiled. "I would buy all of them if it would help me
find someone I'm looking for."

Mrs. Fitzgerald ignored his comment and moved away from
Graham to straighten a shelf. "Please look around. If you need
anything, yell for Mr. Fitzgerald and he will help you."

She scurried away, not giving Graham a chance to ask her
any more questions. He followed her, his steps slow. He didn't
wish to make her more nervous than she already was.

Mr. Fitzgerald stepped out from behind the counter once he saw Graham following his wife. "A returning customer. What can we help you find today?"

While following Mrs. Fitzgerald to the counter, he noticed the shop sat empty and got to the point. His patience had run out. "I'm looking for Sabrina. Have you seen her today?"

The Fitzgeralds exchanged a look before Mrs. Fitzgerald declared, "We are sorry, sir. We are unfamiliar with anyone by that name."

Graham laid his palms on the counter. "Please, I need your help."

Mr. Fitzgerald narrowed his gaze and stared at Graham with suspicion, as if he were the one responsible for Sabrina's injuries. "As my wife stated, we cannot help you."

Graham tore off his hat, scrunching it in his hand. "Please. I must know how she fares. I wish to help her," he pleaded.

"Are you responsible for the beating she took?" Mrs. Fitzgerald questioned Graham.

Graham hung his head in shame. "I am to blame because of my interest in Sabrina. But I would never harm her, nor would anyone I am associated with."

Mr. Fitzgerald sighed. "We see you are good for her. But I worry your interest will be her death sentence. We only mean to protect her."

"I wish for the same," Graham stated.

Mrs. Fitzgerald wrung her hands together. "She carries a heavy burden of responsibility by protecting everyone Lady L terrorizes. Sabrina will never abandon those she cares for to find her own happiness."

Graham stalked away from the counter to peer out the windows. "I understand, and after tomorrow, all this terror will end. However, I must get a message to Sabrina before then. I need to warn her."

He wandered around the shop, noting the items they carried. Anything needed for the common household lined the shelves. Nothing out of the ordinary stood out to cause these nice people to become victims of Lady Langdale. But then the lady needed no reason to wield her power around. And Sabrina offered them any protection she could so they never had to endure Lady L's wrath.

"How does she help you?" Graham asked.

"She covers any amount we are short to pay with her own funds," Mrs. Fitzgerald explained.

"How? Where does she find the money?"

"We do not know," answered Mr. Fitzgerald.

Graham held his arms out wide. "These payments. Did you borrow money from Lady Langdale for this shop?"

"Loan." Mr. Fitzgerald scoffed. "The woman extorts money from every shopkeeper along this way. We either pay for her protection or she destroys our livelihoods."

Mr. Fitzgerald stalked to the front of the store to finish setting up a display he had started earlier in the day. Graham had frustrated the shopkeeper by discussing Lady Langdale with him. He hadn't realized Lady L's destruction had reached this level, but how else would she hide in plain sight than to threaten everyone within her radius? She guaranteed her protection by their silence.

Graham reached into his suit coat to withdraw a letter he had written to Sabrina. He wanted to leave it with the Fitzgeralds with the hope they could pass it to her without Lady L's knowledge. Before he handed it over to Mrs. Fitzgerald, Mr. Fitzgerald knocked the display he worked on over, spilling the contents in the doorway's path. Someone could still walk in, but he trapped them from moving any farther until he cleaned the mess.

"Mrs. Fitzgerald, it would be in our best interest if you were to show our guest the way to our private residence," Mr. Fitzgerald informed his wife.

His wife didn't need to question the reason behind her husband's suggestion. It meant the subject of their conversation was on her way inside the store. "Follow me."

Mrs. Fitzgerald hurried behind the curtain separating the storage area and the shop. Graham followed her up a set of stairs and into a living area above the store. The sparse area held a small armchair and a dining set comprised of four chairs. Along the hallway, there were two rooms. Graham assumed they were bedrooms.

"Go into the first room and hide in the closet. We will come and get you when it is safe for you to leave. Whatever you do, please stay silent," Mrs. Fitzgerald demanded before rushing back down the stairs.

Graham wanted to peek out the window to catch a look at Lady Langdale. But he didn't dare risk the Fitzgeralds' lives. Was Sabrina with her? He walked into the room and saw it was indeed a bedchamber filled with a bed and a nightstand. He moved into the closet but left the door open a slit so he could hear if anyone entered the apartment. It was better to prepare his defense than sit as a target caught by surprise. Graham slid to the floor and leaned against the wall.

And waited.

Sabrina followed Barbara into the Fitzgeralds' shop. As soon as they stepped inside, a fallen display blocked their path. Mr. Fitzgerald mumbled a variety of curses at the scattered merchandise. When he noticed it was Lady L visiting his shop, his movements grew flustered.

"My apologies, my lady. I will clean this mess right away. I only need a broom. Hold on," the shopkeeper rambled on, picking up the fallen bags of flour.

Mrs. Fitzgerald hurried over to her husband with a broom. "Here you are, Mr. Fitzgerald. Greetings, Lady Langdale, what a surprise. Come this way." She directed them around the mess her husband had created. "How may we help you today?"

Sabrina noticed the slight tremor in Mrs. Fitzgerald's voice, but her stepmother seemed oblivious to it. Barbara held disgust at the mess that greeted them. Sabrina sensed there was more to the Fitzgeralds' behavior than their need not to add to Lady L's wrath. Rumors had swiftly spread of Lady L's unkindness, sending everyone running whenever she drew near.

"My daughter is having tea with a prominent peer tomorrow, and I need her outfitted in a gown to draw everyone's envy. Since you have a few dresses in stock, I will need you to make the alterations this afternoon to one of them to meet my requirements," Barbara demanded.

"Yes, my lady. Let me show you what we have for you to choose from." Mrs. Fitzgerald led Lady Langdale over to the dresses.

Barbara snapped her fingers. "Come along, Sabrina. Do not dally. I have other places to visit this afternoon."

Sabrina obeyed her stepmother because she had no other choice. Since her beating, she had followed every order to avoid the lady's wrath. Her body still ached with every movement. And she struggled not to break down and cry out her misery. Barbara Langdale would never claim victory over breaking her.

"This white dress is lovely, and her hair will highlight her best features," Mrs. Fitzgerald gushed.

Barbara sneered. "White no longer suits my daughter."

Mrs. Fitzgerald looked at Sabrina in sympathy before nervously making her next suggestion. "That only leaves us with these dresses that are bolder."

Barbara tapped her finger against her lips, surveying her choices. She then pointed at the forest-green dress. "That one there."

Mrs. Fitzgerald pulled the dress out to lie on her worktable. "What alterations do you require?"

Barbara stepped toward the table. "Rip off all this lace and make the neckline lower. I want Sabrina's ample bosom on display. Then bring in the dress so it clings to Sabrina's curves." She dropped a silk bag onto the dress. "Then sew these jewels along the neckline and down this row of ribbon." Barbara pointed at the ribbon on the dress that would run from Sabrina's breast down along her stomach.

Her stepmother meant to dress Sabrina like a whore. To embarrass her in front of the ton, especially her new friend Evelyn. But she refused to let her Barbara degrade her when Sabrina held no shame for loving Graham. She would follow the same path again if given the chance.

"If you need this dress by tomorrow, then Sabrina must stay so I can alter the dress as I sew," Mrs. Fitzgerald stated.

Barbara narrowed her eyes at Mrs. Fitzgerald, then swept her gaze around the shop to see if the shopkeeper had another reason to keep her stepdaughter there. However, Mrs. Fitzgerald did not show the fear that racked her.

"Very well. Her presence will only hinder what I need to accomplish today." She turned to Sabrina and threatened her. "I will leave a guard in front and behind this shop. Don't even attempt an escape. They will inform me of every soul who comes or leaves this shop."

Sabrina nodded. Part of her wished Mrs. Fitzgerald didn't make the offer for her to remain because now she wouldn't learn of Barbara's plans for tomorrow. But then relief washed over her at escaping Barbara's clutches for the day. The Fitzgeralds would be a welcoming balm from the terror she had lived in since her beating.

Mr. Fitzgerald walked up behind them, carrying the broom and a bucket filled with the mess he had cleaned. "Do not worry, my lady. We will make sure no one unworthy has contact with Sabrina. She can remain in the backroom with Mrs. Fitzgerald."

Barbara smiled. "Thank you, Mr. Fitzgerald, for understanding my concern for Sabrina. We would not want any more harm to come upon her so soon after her attack."

Mr. Fitzgerald bowed. "We do what we must to serve you, my lady."

Barbara smiled at what she perceived to be their devotion. But Sabrina noticed their underlying demeanor that mocked her instead. However, Barbara was too conceited to notice otherwise. When her stepmother left without another order, Sabrina relaxed for the first time in days. She would endure her visit inside this clustered shop with gratitude since it kept her away from her tortured existence.

"You poor dear. How do you feel today?" Mrs. Fitzgerald asked, wrapping a comforting arm around Sabrina.

Sabrina smiled. "Better now that I am surrounded by friends."

"Well, then let us go share a pot of tea before we start." Mrs. Fitzgerald ushered Sabrina upstairs.

Sabrina followed Mrs. Fitzgerald with slow steps. Her side still ached from the kicking she had received. She stood beside the table, holding her side as her face twisted in pain.

Mrs. Fitzgerald winced at the pain etched on Sabrina's features. "Why do you not rest for a spell while I fix the dress?

I already know your measurements to make the alterations. Once I am finished, I will wake you to try on the dress."

"Are you sure?" Sabrina asked.

"Yes, my dear. I only suggested for you to stay to give you a break."

Sabrina yawned. "A nap would be nice. I do not sleep well at night."

Mrs. Fitzgerald nodded. "No, I do not suppose you do. Use the bed in the first room to rest. We will not bother you until you come downstairs."

Mrs. Fitzgerald disappeared out the door before Sabrina thanked her for her kindness. The Fitzgeralds were like the grandparents she had never had, and she hated the treatment they suffered at the hands of Lady Langdale. Sabrina tried what she could to ease the burden, but Barbara thwarted her every attempt. After tomorrow, she hoped everyone she cared for would no longer live in fear.

Sabrina walked toward the bedchamber at her use. She closed the door, slipped off her shoes, slid out of her clothes, and laid them across the end of the bed. She removed all of her clothing because the rough fabric irritated her wounds and the soft sheets on the bed would offer the comfort she needed.

The sheets felt like heaven when she slid between them. A sigh drifted past her lips as she sank into the mattress. Or at least what Sabrina imagined heaven to feel like. The only missing link to her fantasy was Graham holding her. Sabrina rolled to her side and placed her hands under her head on the pillow. Her eyelids drifted closed, and she slipped into the sleep her body so desperately craved.

Sabrina never heard the closet door open or saw the gentleman of her dreams step out to stand over her. "Ah, love, it tears my heart apart to see what you have endured."

Graham couldn't believe his eyes when Sabrina stepped through the door. The bruises covering her body when she disrobed struck him speechless. He wanted to roar at the injustice delivered upon her. All because she had grabbed a brief moment of happiness for herself to escape a life filled with every terror one only feared.

He grabbed a chair to sit next to the bed while she slept. Graham sat on the edge of the chair, his hands folded together on the bed, fighting the urge to hold her hands. The dark circle under her eyes showed how she never slept. He wouldn't take this nap away from her with his selfish needs. Those very needs had made her suffer enough as it was.

When Sabrina rolled over and kicked the covers off, Graham's hands curled into fists. He wanted to storm out of the shop and unleash his fury on the brutes responsible for the bruises on the woman he loved. He choked back a sob at the torture she had received. Tears dropped from his eyes, and he opened his hands to catch them on his palms. He closed them into fists again, his sorrow fueling his need to seek vengeance.

Graham's heart cried its own sorrow for Sabrina.

Chapter Sixteen

S ABRINA'S EYES FLUTTERED OPEN to find Graham sitting by the bed, crying. "Graham?"

Graham swiped at his eyes. "Sabrina."

She rolled to her side and wrapped her hands around his. "You should not be here."

"I had to find you. Please come with me," Graham pleaded.

Sabrina peeled Graham's fists opened and traced the path of his wet tears along the lines on his palms. "I cannot. Do not ask the impossible from me."

Graham heard the underlying message in Sabrina's denial. It was her plea for him not to make her choose. To understand her decision and stand by her side. As much as it pained him to do so, he would respect her decision. Because he understood more than anyone how much she had sacrificed and her need to achieve her goals.

Sabrina watched the indecision in Graham's gaze. While he might wish to save her, she also understood her need to seek justice for her father's death and for the others who suffered under Lady L's control. She ran her palm over the rough bristles. By not shaving, he showed her how he continued to defy the look of a proper gentleman to please her.

"I love you," Sabrina whispered.

She had to tell him in case she didn't survive tomorrow. Sabrina wasn't a fool not to know what Lady L planned. Her stepmother planned to kill Evelyn Worthington and pin the crime on Sabrina. No matter what connection Sabrina held with the underground world and the Duke of Colebourne, no one held the power to save her. The authorities would accuse her of a crime she had never committed. Sabrina would find herself hung before she even defended herself.

Graham entwined their fingers together. "Do not hold any obligation to return my sentiments. I expressed my love because I was unable to hold back my feelings for you."

Sabrina raised her gaze to his. "And now I wish to express mine."

Sabrina drew the rest of the blanket off her and held out her hand for Graham to join her on the bed. Graham needed no other encouragement to hold her in his arms. He closed the door and propped the chair under the doorknob to prevent anyone from disturbing them. He discarded his clothing, crawled into bed next to Sabrina, and drew her into his embrace.

"I only want to hold you close." Graham kissed the top of Sabrina's head.

Sabrina sighed as she settled against Graham's warmth. A coldness had seeped into her since they parted, and nothing she did helped to ease the bitter chill. But now her body thawed and rejoiced in the warmth of his embrace.

His hand guided gently over her bruises, offering Sabrina comfort with his soft touch. "Do they still pain you?"

"Only at times." Sabrina didn't wish to discuss her injuries but understood how Graham suffered guilt from not protecting her. She wanted to reassure him the best she could.

"I should never have fallen asleep. I should've seen you safely home," Graham choked out.

Sabrina rolled over and settled her palm against his cheek. "I would never have led you to my home again."

"But . . ."

Sabrina pressed her lips to Graham's and softly persuaded him into silence. Life was full of regrets, and Sabrina never allowed herself to ponder over them. Each time she dreamed of a different outcome, it never changed the reality of the situation. Graham must learn to live with his regrets, as she did with hers.

His kiss felt like heaven, and Sabrina only wanted to share their stolen moments together, loving Graham. To allow their problems to disappear for the time being. Her fingers feathered through his hair as she deepened the kiss. Graham was the salvation her soul had searched for all these years. She drank from his lips, hoping his love would give her the strength she needed to survive.

Graham inhaled her desperation into his soul and offered her all the reassurance he could. He rolled her over carefully so as not to add to her injuries and placed a soft trail of kisses along her neck. His fingers whispered across each of her injuries, and he added a soft kiss to help heal the pain she suffered from. Sabrina's hand continued to flutter in his hair while he worshipped her. There wasn't a spot on her delectable body he didn't caress.

Sabrina's soft sighs helped to ease the burden he carried. When he walked away from her today, it would be to honor her wishes and resist every honorable intention he possessed. She needed to finish what she had started. Making this sacrifice for Sabrina drove him mad. He had never felt more helpless than he did now.

His hand closed around her breast, and his tongue softly licked around the bud until it hardened. He closed his lips over it to savor the ripe berry with soft nibbles. Sabrina's hands tightened in his hair. He smiled and moved to the other bud to give it the same pleasure. Sabrina's sighs swiftly changed to moans. He heard the longing in each drawn-out sound.

Sabrina moaned. "Graham."

"Yes, my love?"

"I need to feel your love inside me." Sabrina's soft request undid him.

He rose over her, drawing her lips into a passionate kiss as he slid inside her. Slow and gentle strokes built their need and brought about the revelation of how much they loved one another. Their time together was made up of stolen moments. However, they didn't need a lifetime of knowing each other to understand the depth of their love. Each kiss they shared held the promise of more to come. Each caress they treasured as a testament of hope. Each whispered sigh declared the message of their love.

Sabrina rode the sensational waves of Graham's movements inside her. With each powerful thrust of his need, she arched her body for the full impact of their bodies joining as one. She drew her legs around his hips and clasped her heels against his back. Sabrina clung to Graham, pressing herself as close to him and soaking up as much warmth and strength as she could get from him.

Graham was drowning as the emotions he held for Sabrina overcame him in a rush more powerful than any tidal wave destroying the innocent beauty of the land. He stared down at his siren, watching her features express each level of ecstasy she reached with him inside her. She threw her head back with her eyes barely open. A pink hue decorated her cheeks, and her tongue swiped across her lips each time he pressed his cock deep inside her core. When he pulled out, she would bite at her bottom lip until he filled her again. Then her lips would part with the moans of her desire.

Graham paused above her, hovering on the crest of their passion. Sabrina drew her heavy lids open to stare at the storm raging in Graham's eyes. Her pirate was magnificent as he unleashed his control on the passion surrounding them in its mist. Every burden he held himself responsible for, he abandoned to find the greatest treasure he searched for. Her love. She gave it to him to treasure close to his heart for eternity.

Sabrina wrapped her hand around Graham's neck and tugged his head toward her to kiss him with the fierce need coursing through her. Her tongue lashed out against his with the force of her desire. She dragged her teeth along his bottom lip, softly biting him. Sabrina needed Graham to anchor her against the tidal wave of her emotions that rode to the surface and tipped her over the edge.

Graham felt Sabrina unraveling around him. Her kiss begged for him to save her from her drowning thoughts. He linked their hands, drew them above her head, and softly kissed her lips.

"I will never allow you to drown. My love is the anchoring ship that will ensure us a safe journey to our destiny." Graham slid his cock slowly into Sabrina's tight canal, her wetness soothing the ache that clawed at him to release. But his selfish need to stay inside Sabrina kept him riding the wave of their desire.

Each time Graham thrust his cock inside her, Sabrina tightened around him. Her desire throbbed with an ache she never wanted to end. When his chest rubbed against her nipples, it sent tingles straight to her core. The whimpers escaping her lips were messages to Graham about how she no longer possessed the control she thought she had. She had relinquished it to him.

The waves soon overtook both of them with no warning. It sent them clinging to one another with the desperation of impending loss. Their lips met in a kiss that breathed life into one another, keeping them alive. Graham's fingers tightened around Sabrina's, holding on for dear life. With each thrust, their love exploded around them, leaving them floating on a raft of exquisite bliss.

As the trembling of their bodies settled, Graham gathered Sabrina in his arms. One of his hands still clutched Sabrina's hand, and he rested them on his chest. He stared at them, hoping the simple gesture held the magical solution to their problem. Instead, it only showed Graham how fragile life was. Once he unlaced his fingers from hers, danger would once again surround them and pull them in opposite directions. However, no matter how hard it tried, it would never destroy the force of their love, keeping the bond around them unbreakable.

"My first glance of you was across the theatre," Graham murmured. "You left me spellbound, and by the time I regained my senses, you had disappeared. Then, throughout the season, I caught glimpses of you at one ball after another, and you were always out of my reach. Until finally, luck blessed me with an encounter with a mermaid."

Sabrina's chuckle rumbled against his chest. Otherwise, she stayed silent, soaking up his words.

"A siren who lured me with her twinkling laughter and sense of humor. You never need to use your siren's call to lure me under your spell because every moment I spend with you, I fall even more enamored with you. When Maggie talked about you at breakfast the next morning and I discovered the mermaid was the very *pretty* girl they tried to introduce me to, I wanted to kick myself at how I wasted precious moments of spending time with you."

Sabrina rolled over and propped her hands on Graham's chest. "You wanted nothing to do with *pretty*."

Graham winked at her. "Because pretty is too tame of a word to describe you, my dear. I will need to speak with my sister on her use of descriptive words to describe someone."

Sabrina swatted at him. "Do not dare. Maggie's description flattered me."

This was one of the many reasons he loved Sabrina. She held no clue about the depth of her beauty. Not only on the outside, but on the inside, where it mattered the most. Her generous soul captured his attention. Sabrina always accepted herself for less than she was worth. He wanted to spend a lifetime treasuring her and showing her how lovable she was.

Graham wanted to quote poetry and flatter her with every endearing term he knew. But he needed her to understand he knew every one of her secrets and not one of them changed his opinion of her. Instead, it only strengthened his love for her.

He started talking again. "Then Maggie mentioned your name and everything became crystal clear to me. The very lady I fell in love with was the lost girl I had wondered where she had disappeared to. My soul mate had been within my reach the entire time. She even knocked me over and stole a bag of coins from me. Then there was the time she evaded my grasp by switching identities within a few feet from me."

Sabrina sat up and wrapped the sheet around her. "What did you mean, you wondered about me?"

Graham sat up too and leaned against the headboard. "I learned whatever I could of Lady Langdale, even down to her stepdaughter. What left me confused is how you disappeared and no one questioned what happened to you, like you never existed."

Sabrina lowered her gaze, picking at the sheet. She always knew why everyone forgot about her. But to hear somebody explain she was forgettable hurt more than she cared to admit. "That was how she wanted it. She never liked the attention I received because it took away from her."

Graham never meant to hurt Sabrina's feelings with his explanation. He tipped her chin up. "Even though I had never met you, I never forgot about you."

Sabrina gave a slight shake of her head. "You do not need to pacify me with false statements."

"They are not false," Graham growled. "I searched for you outside of this investigation. But I never found where you vanished to. Every report from Falcone never indicated Lady L had taken you with her."

"I do not understand why you searched for me."

Graham shrugged. "I never understood myself, other than I feared Lady L had harmed you. Perhaps because you were close to the ages of my sisters and I thought how unfair your life turned out. I couldn't fathom how you could survive in the environment Lady L created. Nor did I want you to."

"Before Barbara fled England, I learned my father kept journals detailing Lady L's crimes and how he worked for Colebourne. One night I overheard Barbara boasting to one of her lovers how she had caused my father's death and how she gained control over my inheritance."

Graham frowned. "Why didn't this lover turn her over to the authorities?"

Sabrina pinched her lips. "Because she blackmailed him, leaving him no choice but to stay silent. Then he helped Barbara secure the rights to adopt me. Before we left, I visited Colebourne, and he told me the reason my father had married Barbara was so he could gather enough evidence to secure her imprisonment, if not her death." Sabrina drew a deep breath.

"I informed Colebourne I would continue my father's work. But he made me promise I would pull out when it became too dangerous."

"It is that time, Sabrina," Graham whispered.

Sabrina smiled sadly at Graham. "No, tomorrow will be."

"Tomorrow might be too late."

Sabrina wrapped the sheet tighter. "Everything is set in motion, ready to play out."

Graham swung his legs off the bed and reached for his trousers. "Yes. However, I have added another player to the game to secure the outcome to fall in our favor tomorrow."

Sabrina drew herself up to her knees. "What have you done?"

Graham finished buttoning the placket of his trousers and drew on his shirt. "I made a deal with DeVille to help me end the reign of Lady Langdale's torment."

Sabrina gasped. "You made a deal with the devil himself."

Graham nodded. "That I did."

"Why?" Sabrina cried.

Graham pulled Sabrina up against him and kissed her with his desperation. "For you. I made the deal to secure your freedom. Everything I do is for you."

Sabrina hit her head against his chest over and over, chanting, "Why? Why? Why?"

Graham cupped her cheeks and rested their foreheads together. "Because I love you with all my heart and soul, and I cannot bear to watch you suffer another day."

Sabrina had lost herself to Graham the first moment she laid eyes on him. At the time, she hadn't known who he was other than her soul claimed him. Once she learned how he threatened everything she had sacrificed for, it never altered how she felt. It had only made her want to love him more. He was the salvation she had sought for years. Even now, she was in awe of how much he loved her. What he sacrificed for her. Sabrina had never experienced love this powerful in her life.

As much as she wanted to believe it was as simple as walking away, she knew better. She had to finish this. Not for herself, but for every person who had fallen victim to the cruelty of Barbara Langdale. While Graham had his plan for tomorrow, she also had her own. She desperately wanted to confide in him, but she stayed silent. She needed that element of surprise on her side.

Graham finished getting dressed. Dracott was correct. He couldn't sway Sabrina. She was bound and determined to arrive at the tea shoppe tomorrow and follow Lady L's plan. He didn't regret telling her their plans. He wanted to show Sabrina he made his sacrifices because of the love he held for her.

Graham lifted Sabrina's dress off the bed and motioned for her to rise. Sabrina stood, dropping the sheet, and Graham dressed her with a tenderness that made Sabrina want to cry. But she didn't. Instead, she soaked up the memories to cherish later as she faced coming to terms with her fears. Once Graham had finished buttoning her dress, he peeled Sabrina's hand open. After reaching into his pocket, he dropped an item into Sabrina's hand and closed her hand into a fist again.

Graham pulled Sabrina in for one last kiss filled with tenderness, devotion, and love. A kiss that left Sabrina in tears. "I love you, Sabrina. If I see you wearing this tomorrow, I will know how your heart beats strong for us."

Before Sabrina responded, Graham left her. She opened her hand and saw the clip she had worn with her mermaid costume. She had left it behind the night they escaped to a new hideout. "Graham?"

When he didn't answer her, she ran out of the bedchamber to catch him. Sabrina needed to warn him about the danger lurking outside. She ran down the staircase and searched the store, but she didn't see him anywhere.

"Did you have a nice rest?" Mrs. Fitzgerald asked.

Sabrina fell onto the chair behind the counter. "Where did he go?"

Mrs. Fitzgerald stitched the jewels on the dress. "Who, dear?"

Sabrina sighed. "It does not matter. He is gone."

She opened her palm, tracing her fingers over the sequins. What he wished for was easy enough for Sabrina to show tomorrow with no hesitation. She would pin it in her hair for Graham to see she held the same powerful emotions for him as he did about her. As soon as he saw what she had planned for tomorrow, he would understand why she remained behind today.

"You should have let him take you with him." Mrs. Fitzgerald shook out the dress after she had finished sewing.

Sabrina smiled wistfully. "I cannot run away from those I care about for my own selfishness."

Mrs. Fitzgerald rested her hand on Sabrina's shoulder. "Perhaps it is time for you to do so."

Sabrina squeezed her hand. "I promise I will after tomorrow."

Her friend nodded at the hair clip Sabrina held. "He has excellent taste."

Sabrina frowned. "This is one he found I wore with my mermaid costume."

Mrs. Fitzgerald shook her head. "No, those were each a rainbow of colors. That one only has green sequins on it. He purchased it that day you snuck out in your boy's costume."

Sabrina tipped her head back and laughed. Even when she thought he held not a clue to who she was, he had known all along. Just as he told her abovestairs. There were no secrets between them anymore. That alone lifted a heavy weight off her shoulders. She hated to deceive him. And today he spoke from the heart and what had she done? She had refused to listen to how strongly he loved her.

When he chose the hair clip, it was as if he held a premonition of what was to happen. It matched her dress perfectly.

"I need you to make one more adjustment to the dress," Sabrina stated.

"I already have, my dear. And Mr. Fitzgerald has what you require. Now shall we try on the dress?" Mrs. Fitzgerald held the garment out.

Sabrina changed into the dress, and her appearance astonished her. Mrs. Fitzgerald had taken a simple day dress and turned it into a magnificent gown, outfitted for a day of danger. The hidden pocket Sabrina required was the perfect size to fit her needs.

Her hand ran along the jewels. "Do you think these are real?"

Mrs. Fitzgerald moved around the small room, cleaning the mess she had made. "They appear so, but I am sure they are fake. If not, then you, my dear, shall be wearing a small fortune tomorrow."

Sabrina cringed at the notion. "You are probably correct."

She swiftly changed so Mr. Fitzgerald could wrap the gown and the other item Sabrina required for tomorrow before Lady Langdale returned. Sabrina sat on a chair, waiting for her stepmother with the package on her lap. Once the guard stepped into the shop, she hugged Mrs. Fitzgerald before she left. She didn't know if she would see the woman she had grown to care for after tomorrow. It all depended on how the game played out.

Hopefully, it all ended tomorrow.

Chapter Seventeen

GRAHAM SNUCK INTO THE nursery to play with Mina, hoping to avoid the other members of his family. He found his niece sitting around a small table, hosting a tea party with her dolls. Her governess saw him, and he winked at her, holding a finger to his lips to stay silent, and pointed that she could leave and take a break. She nodded and slipped away without her charge seeing her.

"Today is a splendid day, is it not, Mrs. Potts?" Mina asked her toy.

Graham chuckled as Mina poured Mrs. Potts an imaginary cup of tea. She placed one biscuit on Mrs. Potts's plate and three on hers.

"That is unfair of you to choose three biscuits for yourself and only offer Mrs. Potts one. I am sure she would like two biscuits to eat," Graham reprimanded Mina, tickling her sides.

Mina squirmed to get away, giggling at his silliness. "Gam Gam, you came to play. Will you stay and have tea with us?"

Graham stretched out on the floor. "Only if my friend can join us, too."

Mina pinched her lips, looking around. "What friend?"

Graham reached behind him and drew out the rag doll from underneath his coat. "I thought you might need a new friend to enjoy tea with."

Mina took the doll and hugged her close. "Thank you, Gam."

Graham accepted Mina's hug and tapped her on the nose. "You are welcome, love."

Mina sat the doll on a chair next to Mrs. Potts and placed one of her biscuits on a plate for her new guest. Then she handed the other biscuit to Graham. She bit into the biscuit before asking, "Uncle Gam, did you really meet a mermaid?"

Graham coughed after almost choking on a biscuit. "Yes, I suppose I did." He saw no harm in feeding the child's imagination.

Mina picked up Mrs. Potts and pretended the doll spoke in her ear before setting it back on the chair. "Mrs. Potts has inquired if she is pretty and if you plan to marry her?"

Graham twisted his lips, pondering the questions. "Well, Mrs. Potts, she is more than pretty. She is beyond lovely." Graham looked around the playroom. "Can you and your friends keep a secret?"

Mina nodded with enthusiasm. "Yes. Yes."

Graham leaned close to Mina and her dolls and whispered, "Yes, I plan to ask her to marry me soon."

Mina jumped up and clapped her hands. "Yes! A mermaid in the family. Will she join us for tea soon?"

Graham smiled. "I believe she would love to."

Graham spent the afternoon playing with his niece. Mina's company helped to keep him calm, and she gave him hope for the future. He hoped he would enjoy playing with his own children within a few years. He only needed for tomorrow to come. Then everything standing in the way of his and Sabrina's happiness would vanish, leaving them to create a life together.

He had settled in a rocking chair to read Mina a book. However, soon after he finished two pages, she fell fast asleep in his arms. He closed the book, rested it on the shelf by him, and continued rocking Mina. Soon, Evelyn came to check on her daughter.

Evelyn held out her arms to carry Mina over to her bed, but Graham shook his head no. He wasn't ready to release his precious hold. "I do not mind holding her. I have neglected my uncle duties of late."

Evelyn settled into a chair next to him, gazing at her daughter with motherly devotion. "She has missed you. We all have."

Graham nodded but didn't offer any other reply. His family's deception still stung. It crushed his ego to think his family not only didn't trust him, but they also held no faith in his ability to set his personal feelings aside to bring Lady Langdale to justice.

Evelyn attempted to defend her husband's actions. "The blame lies with Uncle Theo. He is the one who wanted you kept out of the discussion. Reese argued his case for you to be involved from the start. You can even ask Falcone and everyone present about your brother's argument."

Graham stared at Evelyn. He always listened to her sound logic and never resisted her pleading words to forgive Reese. Hell! He had fallen in love with his sister-in-law the first day he met her. She had defied Reese and had gotten under his brother's skin like no one ever had before. He enjoyed watching his brother fall victim to Evelyn's charms. Graham loved Evelyn like a sister and valued her opinion of all things, even though she constantly defended his brother at every turn.

"You make it difficult for me to stay angry with Reese," Graham mumbled.

"It is unfair of me to play on your kindness like I do. However, on this subject, you must understand how your brother defended your loyalty and how proud of you he is. How we all are." Evelyn folded her hands on top of her stomach. "How is Sabrina?"

Graham stopped rocking. "What gives you the belief that I found her?"

Evelyn smiled wistfully. "Because the sadness in your eyes has changed. At first, your expression appears defeated, yet the longer I stare at you, the more I notice a fresh determination stronger than ever. That and you gaze upon Mina with a longing for one of your own. You wouldn't hold that look if you didn't believe there stood a chance for you and Sabrina."

Graham knew exactly where Mina gained her mindfulness. Her mama held the capability to know a person's insight. Perhaps it was why they always got along so well. Evelyn always understood when he wanted to be taken seriously or when he only teased.

"She is recovering but stands firm on remaining with Lady Langdale," Graham admitted.

Evelyn stood and brushed the hair away from her daughter's cheek before pressing a soft kiss on it. Then she kissed Graham's cheek. "Then you must trust in her. Your heart holds faith she has no intention to cause me any harm. All will be well after tomorrow. After you lay Mina down, please visit with Reese."

Evelyn left the nursery after doling out her advice. He wished it was as simple as Evelyn stated, but at this point, he wasn't sure of anything more except for how much he loved Sabrina. Which left him taking Evelyn's advice and placing his trust at Sabrina's mercy. He hoped everything fell into place.

Graham rose, settled Mina on her bed, and pulled the quilt over her small frame. Mina turned on her side, clutching her new doll. After one more longing glance at his niece, he went down the stairs to Reese's study. The door stood open, and when Graham stepped inside, he found Evelyn in Reese's embrace, sharing a kiss.

Graham cleared his throat. "I am sorry to interrupt. Evelyn led me to believe you wished to talk. If I had known you two needed your privacy, I would have respected a closed door. However, since the door remained open, I assumed it was all right to walk in."

Reese shook his head at Graham's sarcasm, and Evelyn blushed bright red at what she considered his teasing. She stepped out of Reese's embrace and started toward the door.

When she reached Graham, she swatted him on the arm and mumbled, "You are incorrigible, mister."

Graham pecked Evelyn on the cheek. "And you would not have me any other way."

Evelyn chuckled. "No, we would not."

Evelyn closed the door, leaving Graham to face Reese in silence. He expected his brother to frown and settle behind his desk. However, Reese surprised Graham by walking up to him and grabbing him by his shoulders.

"I apologize for not standing up to Colebourne and demanding your presence at the start of the meeting. I want you to know how proud I am of what you have accomplished these past years. You hold my utmost trust, and you will succeed in the capture of Lady Langdale." Reese squeezed Graham's shoulders, emphasizing his point before dropping his arms.

Graham patted Reese on the arm before settling in an armchair by the fireplace. "Thank you for your support."

Reese sat in the chair opposite him. "I never should have allowed Colebourne the authority in my own home."

Graham shrugged. "I understand. With Colebourne, you are stuck in the middle with Evelyn. You and every other person in London and beyond."

Reese winced at Graham's sarcasm. "Yes. He has a tight hold on many people."

Graham sat forward in his chair, clasping his hands between his knees. "I only ever wanted to gain your respect. It stung my pride when I walked in to find everyone involved left me out of something I had worked so hard to achieve."

"We never intended to exclude you. We worried your involvement with Sabrina left you vulnerable to Lady Langdale and your feelings would jeopardize the investigation," Reese explained.

"I understand."

Reese blew out his breath. "But it showed our lack of faith in you, and for that, I am deeply ashamed. Because you've done everything to show us you would never betray the investigation. No matter how strongly you feel about Sabrina."

Graham scoffed. "And yet today I've done that very thing."

"How so?"

"I found Sabrina, and I told her of our plan for tomorrow," Graham confessed.

"Excellent."

Graham's eyebrows crinkled. "Excellent?"

Reese leapt to his feet and moved behind the chair, gripping the back of it. "Yes. Honesty must exist between you two if you are to survive through this ordeal. Do you trust Sabrina?"

"Yes." There was not an ounce of doubt in Graham's reply.

"Then when tomorrow is upon us, you have prepared Sabrina. There will be no element of surprise for her when we destroy Barbara Langdale and end this nightmare once and for all," Reese rationalized.

Graham peered at his brother skeptically. "You seem confident in tomorrow's success."

"As should you."

Graham sat, pondering his brother's comment. While he walked around with a bruised ego at his family's betrayal, he also allowed his own doubt to settle in. He let every insecurity he held overtake his faith in himself. Reese was correct. Tomorrow would be a success. He had made sure of every probable outcome and had planned accordingly. He might have sold a part of his soul to the devil to accomplish success tomorrow, but once he held Sabrina in his arms and they destroyed Barbara Langdale, it would make it all worth it.

Graham stood tall. "I do."

He reached his hand out to his brother in an act to show he forgave him, but Reese wanted no part of the simple act. He wrapped Graham in a brief hug before stepping back.

"I appreciate your guidance all these years and your belief in me."

Reese smiled. "You've never had to gain my respect, Graham. Because you've always had it." Reese walked over to pour them each a glass of whiskey. "Now my patience, that is another story."

Graham took a sip. "No need to thank me. It has been a pleasure to annoy you throughout the years."

Reese scowled. "I do not believe I offered my gratitude."

Graham laughed. "I know."

Reese chuckled. "My wife is correct. You are incorrigible." Reese took a drink. "I must express my gratitude toward you, though."

Graham appeared confused. "For what exactly?"

Reese smirked. "Of the immense pleasure I found in watching you fall. Also, I shall enjoy watching you chase the lovely Sabrina."

Graham scoffed. "I will not have to chase Sabrina."

Reese chuckled. "Oh, you have much to learn. I cannot wait to share this with the family at dinner."

Graham frowned at being the subject of his brother's amusement. He threw the whiskey back and set the glass on Reese's desk. He growled in annoyance at Reese's continuous laughter and stalked to the door. Graham refused to sit through dinner with his family laughing at his expense.

"I will see you tomorrow," Graham muttered, opening the door.

He almost ran into his mother, Evelyn, and his sisters, who were eavesdropping at the door. Graham shook his head at their antics and continued on his way, especially after Reese urged them inside.

"You will not believe what Graham said," Reese bellowed.

Graham should have stayed with Mina. At least his niece thought he hung the moon and did no wrong.

Why wouldn't Sabrina too?

Chapter Eighteen

SABRINA STROLLED INTO THE Tea and Crumpet Tea Shoppe with confidence she far from felt. However, she had perfected how to alter her appearance differently from her mood. If she displayed her emotions at the moment, she would be a bumbling mess.

A sense of calm had settled over her yesterday after Graham left. She had held faith today would end with everyone declaring victory at Barbara Langdale's demise and the few people left who still supported her.

However, she had lost her faith when Barbara threatened not only her but everyone who mattered to her, too. Now doubt and fear consumed Sabrina. She had spent the entire evening pacing back and forth in her bedchamber and running through several scenarios on how events would play themselves out.

By morning, Sabrina had regained her faith and prepared herself accordingly. Until her stepmother forced Sabrina to dress in front of her and wouldn't leave her side until they left for Mayfair. Her plan unraveled and slipped away.

Sabrina hid the weapon Mr. Fitzgerald had wrapped with the gown under the mattress. But since Barbara watched her dress, she couldn't hide the knife in the secret compartment

Mrs. Fitzgerald had sewn in the dress. On the carriage ride, her stepmother never spoke a word, only stared at Sabrina with suspicion.

Once they reached their destination, Barbara issued one more warning that still rang in Sabrina's ears. "Make one false move, and my guards will carry out my threats."

A shiver ran along Sabrina's spine, but she remained poised with a smile on her face. She only hoped Evelyn believed it to be genuine. Evelyn struggled to her feet and waved her hand in the air for Sabrina to see her. She rushed forward so Evelyn could rest again. A stabbing sensation kept slicing through her conscience about how Evelyn might come to harm. Sabrina wouldn't be able to live with herself if so. She must make it her mission to protect Evelyn from any harm.

Evelyn greeted Sabrina. "I am so thrilled you've come. I thought perhaps I might have scared you away with my eagerness to become friends."

Sabrina smiled. "No. I've looked forward to our visit all week."

Evelyn beamed. "Excellent. I hope you do not mind, but I've ordered our tea and some sandwiches. You can choose the dessert."

Sabrina laughed. "Well, then I hope you enjoy chocolate."

Evelyn spread the napkin on her lap. "'Tis my favorite sweet."

Sabrina watched Evelyn pour the tea into their cups. She kept smiling, even though she wanted to frown. Something appeared different about Evelyn, and Sabrina tried to figure out what it was. Other than her friend appeared more forceful than the Evelyn she conversed with before. While Evelyn had been eager for them to visit, she hadn't been pushy.

She took a swift peek around the tea shoppe without making it obvious as she surveyed her surroundings. Most of the occupants enjoyed a brief respite from their shopping or they visited with friends. However, she saw two of Lord Kincaid's men. A sense of relief settled over Sabrina at the protection they offered Evelyn, but the impending doom still kept her on edge.

Evelyn reached out to pat Sabrina's hand. "Now tell me, how are you enjoying the season thus far?"

Sabrina frowned as she noticed a difference in the lady that made her question who she sat with. But it must be Evelyn because her twin sister had returned to her estate for the rest of the season. Nor was she pregnant. "It has been most pleasant."

Evelyn tilted her head to the side and perused Sabrina as if she tried to decide if Sabrina was worth the hassle. Then she leaned forward to whisper, "Is it because of Graham?"

Sabrina blushed. She wasn't aware his family had learned of their relationship. But when Evelyn winked, Sabrina realized they were aware of what had transpired between them. She glanced away, trying to maintain her control, then turned back to stare into Evelyn's eyes. However, when she noticed how the lady held a different eye color, she realized Evelyn didn't sit across from her. Charlotte Sinclair did. This changed everything.

Sabrina took a bite of the sandwich to appear as if they discussed the mundane events of the season. "Your carelessness to not cover every detail when you switched identities will ruin the plan Graham has sacrificed everything for."

Her companion patted at her lips with the napkin. "And what might those be?"

Sabrina continued with the act and took a sip of tea. "I commend you on your performance. It is obvious how easily you have fooled others before with the switch. However, those who are clever at the art of disguises can spot the differences immediately." Sabrina smiled. "I will admit my attention became distracted when I first arrived, Charlie. May I call you Charlie? Or should we keep up with the pretense of addressing you as Evelyn?"

Charlie sat back in the chair with a smug expression. "He said you were clever and wouldn't fall for the ruse. So what should we have done differently?"

The he, Charlie referred to, could only be Graham. His understanding of how her mind worked gave her the courage she lacked when she had first walked inside. "First, your behavior was a bit pushy. Second, your wedding ring is a sapphire whereas Evelyn's is an emerald. And of course, the crucial clue was one too impossible to alter."

Charlie nodded. "Our eye color."

"Mmm. Yes."

The gentleman walking toward them distracted Sabrina from her conversation with Charlie. He strode toward them with confidence, and the smile on his face showed his pleasure at seeing her. Sabrina's heart took off in a race she didn't believe would ever slow down.

Graham greeted them. "Evelyn, how wonderful to run into you. And, Lady Sabrina, what a joy to see you again."

Charlie invited him to sit down. "Please join us. Sabrina and I were having the most magnificent conversation, and I would love to judge your opinion on the matter."

Graham pulled a chair to their table and sat in between them. "It would be my pleasure."

Graham absorbed every nuance of Sabrina. She looked as glorious today as she had yesterday in the plainest of dresses. He didn't fathom why Maggie had referred to her as pretty, when clearly she was the loveliest lady to grace the world. He drew his eyes to her hair. She wore the ribbon he had snuck into her reticule braided through her locks. Also nestled in her raven locks was the hair clip he'd given her before he left. The green sequins glistened in the sunlight, giving him the hope he had wished for all morning.

"You look so lovely, Sabrina," Graham whispered.

Sabrina lifted her hand, then settled it back on her lap. "You shaved."

Her fingers itched to wrap around and caress his smooth cheek. He was even more magnificent with a shaven face than he was with the bristles that scraped her whenever they kissed. She felt a wave of warmth flush over her face at where her thoughts traveled to. What she loved most about the whiskers was how he inflamed her desires each time they scraped across her thighs as his mouth made love to her.

He leaned forward for only Sabrina to hear. "Only for today. I will grow them again for a chance at your gentle touch."

Charlie cleared her throat. "As happy as I am some lady finally brought you to your knees, I prefer not to listen to the intimate details. It was awful enough I had to watch Evelyn and Reese kiss at breakfast."

Graham shuddered. "I walked in on them in the study yesterday."

Charlie rolled her eyes. "They have no shame."

Graham laughed. "I agree."

Sabrina's gaze bounced back and forth between their amicable discussion of Reese and Evelyn Worthington. It astonished her how they discussed their intimacy as a source of amusement. When her gaze landed on Graham again, she realized that, while he joked with Charlie, he never glanced away from her once. Her eyes soaked him in, taking in his black suit with a green vest and cravat. And clipped to his pocket was the hair clip she had left behind for him to find.

The rainbow sequins told her a story of their own. Graham declared he trusted her and stood behind her decision, while she wore the hair clip to express how she believed in their love. They both offered their statements of loyalty to one another.

"I think they are quite the romantic couple," Sabrina interjected, and they groaned at her comment.

"We must keep her away from Uncle Theo," Charlie quipped Graham winked at Sabrina. "Most definitely."

"So what is our next step?" Charlie asked.

Graham slid his hand under the table to grasp Sabrina's hand. "Sabrina will guide us on how we are to proceed."

Sabrina looked up in surprise. "I will?"

Graham squeezed her hand, showing his faith in her ability to guide them to victory. "Yes, you will."

"I am to lead Evelyn out of the shoppe and toward my carriage, offering her a ride home."

Charlie frowned. "But I have my own carriage to take."

"Yes. However, you will send your carriage away because we have decided to shop for the new babe. Then we will proceed to enter a shoppe two places to the left of here, where Lady Langdale is lying in wait to act on her revenge," Sabrina explained.

"That is a simple problem to solve. I will get men in position to storm the shoppe. This nightmare is almost over." Graham stood.

Sabrina touched his sleeve. "'Tis not as simple as it seems."

Graham should've known better. There was no simple situation concerning Lady Langdale. "What does she have planned?"

"If she does not arrive back at the hideout by a particular time, then the guards will initiate the next step in her plans. Also, there is a guard who awaits across the street for any sign of an ambush. If he sees Lady L is under attack, he is to run and inform the guard to proceed as planned," Sabrina finished.

"What else?" Graham growled.

Sabrina squeezed her hands together on top of the table. "She has the Fitzgeralds tied up in their shoppe. The guards have instructions to set their shoppe on fire."

"Damn her," Graham swore. "She has made it impossible for you to defy her."

Sabrina nodded.

"Do you trust me?" Graham asked Sabrina.

Tears gathered in Sabrina's eyes. "With my life."

Graham turned to Charlie. "Sinclair will string my arse up for this, but are you willing to take this a step further?"

Charlie quirked an eyebrow up. "Need you ask?"

"Can you point out the guard across the way?" Graham asked.

Sabrina scowled. "Aye. He is the one who beat me."

A sinister smile spread across his face. He thought he would never get his revenge. Graham would find much pleasure in torturing Sabrina's abuser. He grabbed Sabrina's hand, tugged her to her feet, and walked them over to the window. "Point him out."

Sabrina turned back to the table, looking around the tea shoppe to see who watched them. But no one glanced their way. Still, she couldn't afford to have any word get back to Lady Langdale of her talking with Graham. "I must return to my seat."

Graham turned Sabrina back to him and lifted her chin. "Look at me." Sabrina raised her gaze to his, but her gaze kept darting around. "Everyone inside here either works alongside me or for DeVille. They are here to protect you."

Sabrina took another look around. She had failed to notice her surroundings with her nerves on edge to protect Evelyn, then Graham had distracted her when he walked in. The number one mistake to make and she did so today. While she recognized Lord Kincaid's guards protecting Evelyn, she had paid little attention to the other visitors. The occupants in the shoppe were DeVille's people, and the other tables were filled with members of Graham and Evelyn's family. Sabrina had even missed seeing Graham's business partner sitting in the corner with his wife. How had she missed the obvious? It was because she focused her attention on getting Evelyn to comply with her wishes so she could save the Fitzgeralds. Now she not only risked their lives, but she also risked Charlie's life too.

Sabrina finally realized it was impossible for her to destroy Barbara alone. There were too many lives at stake to risk taking Lady Langdale down by herself. She must admit defeat and pray Graham had a plan for them to succeed.

Sabrina pointed at the scruffy guard dressed in shabby clothing with his hat pulled low over his eyes. He had propped himself against a building and chewed on a piece of straw. A chill ran through her as she stared at her tormenter. "There he is."

Graham wrapped a comforting arm around Sabrina and led her back to her seat. "I will take care of him myself."

Sabrina clung to his arm. "No," she cried.

"I will come to no harm, my love," Graham promised.

"Please don't," Sabrina pleaded. "You do not understand how brutal he can be."

"I will not attempt to grab him on my own. I will take reinforcements along," Graham tried to reassure Sabrina.

Graham waved Ralston over to the table and explained their dilemma. Ralston looked out the window at the guard and sat down. "One of Kincaid's men is roughly the same size. After we cause a commotion in front of the shoppe Lady Langdale waits in, we can knock him out. After we swap out their clothes, Lady Langdale won't even realize the difference."

"Leave him for me to deal with," Graham growled.

Ralston slapped him on the back. "With pleasure, my friend."

Ralston joined Kincaid at his table to relay the plan, then he gathered Gemma and left the tea shoppe. It wasn't long before a group gathered outside the shoppe and Sabrina heard shouting. They sat at the table, waiting in silence for the signal that would affirm the plan had worked. After the crowd thinned out, Ralston came in through the back door and nodded at Graham. It was a success.

Charlie drummed her fingers on the table. "Now?"

"I will need you to follow Sabrina's order. After you enter the shoppe, we will surround it and take Lady L down. Then, once we have secured her capture, Sabrina can lead us to the hideout, where we will finish this once and for all," Graham ordered.

Charlie tilted her head to the side, pinching her lips as she debated if the plan was solid enough to follow through. "Let's finish this. We wait much longer and Jasper will ruin everything."

Graham drew Sabrina into his arms. "It is almost over, my love."

Sabrina clutched at his lapels and whispered, "Barbara expects me to kill Evelyn and take the fall. You cannot send Charlie in with me, 'tis a death trap for her."

"We will intervene before it even reaches that point," Graham promised.

Charlie hooked her arms through Sabrina's. "Come on. We can handle that bitch together. I've been wanting to punch her since I first heard of her."

In trying to keep up with Charlie, Sabrina bumped into the tables and chairs in their way. "I do not think someone in your condition is to move as swiftly as you are."

Charlie scoffed. "But I am not in this condition."

"No. But Evelyn is, and you are supposed to portray her," Sabrina pointed out.

"Yes. I know, but if I slow down any, then he will catch us." Charlie nodded toward Reese Worthington, who stalked toward them with a scowl.

Sabrina grimaced. "Perhaps we should let him have his say."

Charlie shook her head rapidly. "Not a wise idea at all. Now pick up your skirts and hurry along."

She left Sabrina with no choice but to follow.

Chapter Nineteen

C HARLIE AND SABRINA MADE their way out the door and past one shoppe. Then, before they realized it, Reese Worthington stormed past them, turned, and blocked their path. Even though they rushed, it wasn't fast enough.

"No! Absolutely not!" Worthington roared.

Sabrina cringed, standing behind Charlie. "He is correct. You must not follow me."

Worthington pointed at her. "My order includes you, too."

Charlie shoved back at Worthington. "You hold no authority over me, Worthington."

Worthington barked out a laugh. "As a matter of fact, I do. Sinclair made it very clear I was to stop you from doing anything foolish, no matter what."

Charlie wormed her way out of his grasp and continued to the shoppe they needed to enter. She rested her hand on her swollen belly and called out, "Was this the shoppe you mentioned, Sabrina?"

Sabrina panicked, glancing back and forth between Charlie and Worthington. Charlie smirked, reaching for the door handle while Sabrina swore steam rushed out of Worthington's ears. The scowl on his face deepened, and his face turned red in fury. If she didn't answer Charlie, then the lady risked coming to harm. But if she defied Worthington's order, she feared what he might do. However, as Barbara peeked out the window, it became clear what Sabrina must do. She had no choice but to follow Charlie into the store.

"I am sorry, Lord Worthington. She has left me with no other choice," Sabrina mumbled, then called out, "Wait for me, Evelyn. My shoe slipped off and I need to repair it."

Charlie kept up an animated discussion about shoes once she saw a lady watching her from inside the shoppe. "Those darn ribbons, they always catch, do they not?"

"Damn her. She has been a thorn in my side ever since I married Evelyn. She cannot listen to reason and jumps in without thinking." Worthington took Sabrina's elbow and guided them forward. "Follow my lead, my dear. This is something I should have taken care of a long time ago. Then perhaps it wouldn't have progressed as far as it had."

"I do not think it would have made a difference, Lord Worthington," Sabrina said.

"Reese. But we shall become better acquainted later." He smiled at her before turning his scowl back on Charlie.

"Oh, Reese, darling. How kind of you to help Sabrina. I didn't know you were in the area," Charlie gushed.

Worthington wrapped his arm around Charlie, pressing a kiss to her cheek. "When you mentioned you were taking tea with Sabrina today, I thought I would join you." He lowered his voice and hissed, "Turn around. We are leaving."

Charlie's voice rose. "You missed tea. Now we are shopping for the new babe. After we finish in this shoppe, we can go home." Charlie lowered her voice to hiss at Reese. "No!"

Before their argument continued, the door opened, causing Charlie to fall forward since her hand still clutched the door handle. Worthington saved her from falling, but it forced them both to enter the shoppe, which left Sabrina to follow them. As soon as she stepped inside, the door slammed behind her, and Barbara's guard moved into place, blocking them from leaving. Another guard moved to sweep the curtains closed.

Then Barbara sauntered forward, swishing her hips back and forth. If she thought it made her look attractive, she couldn't be more mistaken. Sabrina snuck a glance at Worthington to see he wore a look of disgust. Whatever they had shared in the past clearly remained so on his part. However, Barbara thought if she disposed of Evelyn, they would resume where they had left off.

Barbara reached out to trail her hand down Worthington's chest, but he swiped her hand away. "Do not touch me."

Barbara's eyes narrowed, and her lips turned up into a snarl. "You never used to utter those words. If I distinctly remember, you used to beg for my touch."

"Akh." Charlie shuddered.

Sabrina lifted her hand to cover her smile. This wasn't progressing how she had imagined. While she should worry over Charlie's reaction to Barbara, she noticed Evelyn's sister stood with confidence that Sabrina was envious to possess.

Barbara turned to glare at who she believed to be Evelyn. "Excuse me?"

Charlie stepped forward. "You heard me correctly." She walked around Lady Langdale in a slow circle, rubbing her stomach in hopes it would irritate Barbara. "What my *husband* found pleasing with you is beyond me," Charlie went on in a dramatic tone. "Obviously his taste leaned toward the . . ." She paused. "How would you describe it, my love?" Charlie batted her eyelashes at Worthington.

"Stop it," Worthington whispered.

"Why, my love? Does this woman not deserve a rebuke for speaking in an intimate nature with you in my presence?" Charlie asked.

Worthington pulled Charlie away from Barbara and held her behind him. "She does, my love," he gritted out between his teeth. "However, not now."

Barbara narrowed her gaze at the couple before focusing on Sabrina. "You've done well, my dear. Not only have you brought the missus, but you've brought me my darling Reese. And here I worried you would betray me. Especially after I saw Graham enter the tea shoppe. You must have been very convincing." She paused, staring back at Charlie and frowning. "Perhaps too much."

Barbara focused her attention on Charlie again and walked in a circle around the couple. Sabrina took them in and noticed how stiffly Worthington held Charlie. For a caring husband, he appeared to show his displeasure at touching his sister-in-law. Not convincing when they were to portray themselves as husband and wife. Then there was Charlie, trying to wiggle away from him. She needed to distract Barbara. But how?

Sabrina stepped forward and grabbed Barbara's arm. "I've accomplished my task and have delivered Evelyn to you. Now I demand you release the Fitzgeralds."

Barbara gave a pointed look at Sabrina's hand, but Sabrina kept her hold firm. She must keep her attention away from Reese and Charlie. If she had to sacrifice herself to keep Barbara from realizing it wasn't Evelyn, then it was worth it. Barbara raised her hand and snapped her fingers, bringing the guards from the front of the shoppe to her side. Sabrina flinched when the guards hovered over her, but she never moved. However, Barbara sighed in disgust and jerked her arm away.

"You are in no position to demand anything," Barbara snarled. "We are far from finished. After I speak with your new friend, then you must accomplish one more task for me."

When Barbara turned back to the Worthingtons, Sabrina hurried over and stepped in her path, blocking them from her view. "You never mentioned another task."

Barbara laughed. "If I had, you would never have brought Lady Worthington to me."

"Please, let her go," Sabrina pleaded.

"What is your intention?" Reese roared.

Barbara shoved Sabrina to the side and nestled up to Reese, sliding her hands along his chest. "My daughter graciously brought your wife to me to win my affection. Sabrina understands how much I wish for your wife's death and has agreed to offer her help in doing so. It was her idea to befriend Evelyn and lure her today so I may watch."

"No!" Sabrina shouted.

At Sabrina's outburst, the guards covered her mouth and held her between them. This was only a warning. Sabrina knew if she didn't stay quiet, it would only get worse for her.

"Is this true?" Reese asked, glaring at Sabrina.

Barbara never gave Sabrina a chance to defend herself. She continued in her attempt to seduce Reese. She trailed her fingers across his cheek, and he recoiled to get out of her reach. "I would never lie to you, my love. She came home excited after a ball and bragged about how she befriended Evelyn and fooled you and your family with her innocence. I informed her she played a dangerous game. However, she only laughed at how everyone was clueless about her identity. Then I warned what may befall her. But you know children, they must defy their parents."

Sabrina shook her head, dislodging the guards' hands. "You are not my mother," Sabrina spat.

Barbara shook her head, smiling with false sweetness at Sabrina. "Yes, I am. I have the paperwork to prove so." She turned back to Reese. "Now, if you will please step aside, my love, I would like to speak with your wife."

Reese backed away from Barbara, urging Charlie to the door since the guards no longer stood near it. "Never. You are mad."

Barbara followed them. "It never bothered you before. In fact, you found my madness intoxicating between the bedsheets. Mmm. Those were some memorable evenings. I cannot wait to experience them with you again. You were skillful in stroking my desires with your prowess." She laughed. "Why, I was only comparing your prowess the other day with Sabrina after she spent a night allowing your brother to ruin her."

"Oh my. Disgusting." Charlie made a gagging sound. "Yes. We get it. You had past relations with Reese. Hence the word past. Must we listen to the details?"

"Silence," Reese ordered.

However, Charlie refused to listen to her brother-in-law. She was finished listening to this shrew. She didn't understand what all the fuss was about her. Charlie didn't see her as a dangerous villain but a diabolical looney who still had an obsession with Reese. She shuddered at the class her brother-in-law had before he married her sweet sister. The gentleman must have had serious issues to work through to entwine himself with this lady.

"No. I will not. This lady spouts lies and plans to implicate Sabrina in this downfall for her own selfish reasons. Now, I ask, what type of mother is this? One who has a vindictive agenda set out to destroy innocent people to cover her flaws. For shame, Lady Langdale, for not being clever enough to achieve your revenge." Charlie stepped away from Reese and smoothed out her skirts.

Sabrina's eyes widened, and she bit back a gasp. Charlie had removed the padding from beneath her dress while she hid behind Reese. Charlie stood with her hands on her hips, daring Barbara to come after her. Sabrina didn't know whether to roll over laughing or warn Charlie about Barbara's wrath. Sabrina watched fury overtake her stepmother.

Barbara Langdale stood with her hands closing into fists and her face turning an ugly shade of red. Sabrina had seen no one outwit Barbara into a state of silence before. The growling noise coming from her wasn't a promising sign for anyone.

"You fool!" The slander echoed before Barbara stormed across the shoppe to slap Sabrina across the face. However, Barbara's rant had only just begun. "You dare to double-cross me? Even when I have your precious Fitzgeralds waiting to meet their demise. Do you believe the Worthingtons will accept you after they learn every detail of how you spent the past few years? They will find disgust with every damaging detail before they turn you over to the authorities. Do you not see how you are part of their ploy? They played you to get to me. Have you not learned anything from me?"

The guards stepped away as Barbara inflicted Sabrina with her own version of terror. She degraded Sabrina with each slanderous comment. "You are a worthless whore now. Graham Worthington will not marry you any more than his brother would've married me. You suited only one purpose for him, and that was to spread your legs so he could ride you all night long. Did he promise you marriage when his head was between your thighs? Or perhaps when you were on your knees, sucking his cock?"

Sabrina paled at the crudeness of her words. Barbara degraded the moments Sabrina had spent in Graham's arms. No. He had never mentioned marriage or a happily ever after. However, Graham had expressed his love. An expression

Sabrina treasured and put her faith in for their future. It was an unspoken promise Barbara would never steal from her.

Reese stepped in between them. "That is enough. Your tyranny of Sabrina is over. We should never have left her to your vices. There are many who were negligent in her welfare, myself included. However, that all ends today."

"She had one simple task to accomplish," Barbara muttered, ignoring Reese's demand.

"If you thought to kill my wife and I would welcome you with open arms, you were mistaken."

Barbara threw her shoulders back, regaining her confidence. Her plans were falling apart, but she still had more cards to play. She perused Reese with distaste. "Yes. I can see how I erred with you. You are not the gentleman I remember. You've become too proper. Also, Sabrina is not your concern." She reached out and patted Reese's cheek. "Terribly sorry, but I'm afraid you will meet your demise today and not Evelyn. However, what better revenge on my part than killing her husband and her sister? This will cause Evelyn much distress. She will spend the rest of her life living with the guilt of causing your deaths."

With a snap of her fingers again, the guards grabbed Reese and Charlie, holding them captive. Charlie kicked and scratched at her captives, while Reese swung his fist out to clip the guard's chin. However, they were no match against the brutes' strength.

Barbara walked up to Charlie. "I must compliment you on your deception. For a while there, you were quite believable. Until you opened your mouth. Then you displayed how unladylike you are with your behavior. A complete opposite of your sister Evelyn, who is sweet and kind. But then what does one expect from a lady who wears breeches and rides a horse like a man?"

With a huge grin on her face, Charlie tilted her head, not frightened by the brute holding her arms behind her back. "A compliment from the villainous Lady Langdale."

Charlie's indifference only infuriated Barbara more. However, she fascinated Sabrina. Her wit alone was swift and damaging. Sabrina must remember to never irritate Charlotte Sinclair.

"Make it look like a lover's spat. Discard their clothes before you kill them. Stab Lord Worthington to death and choke the bitch. You may take your pleasure with her before you end her life. Then leave through the back. I will send word to the authorities of the nefarious activity taken place here. They shall find the scene of Lord Worthington's affair with his sister-in-law." She gasped dramatically. "A horrid scandal that will ruin such prominent families of the ton. Oh, Sabrina, this is craftier than anything I ever planned. Perhaps I might allow the Fitzgeralds to live after all."

Barbara turned and walked toward the back entrance, with the guards pulling Sabrina after her. She glanced over her shoulder, but the other guards blocked her view of Charlie and Reese. What had she done? She had brought about two more deaths at her hands. All for what? The evidence she gathered to destroy Barbara Langdale wouldn't bring her father back to her. Why hadn't she listened to Dracott and left when he pleaded with her to? Barbara was correct. She was exactly like her. In her need to seek revenge against her stepmother and bring Barbara to justice, she had risked so many lives. Sabrina was no better than Barbara. They both sought revenge for different reasons. But revenge was revenge, no matter what form it took.

"Take my life instead. Allow them to leave," Sabrina offered.

"No!" Reese and Charlie shouted at once.

Barbara stopped and slowly turned. She didn't speak but stared over at Reese and Charlie, then back at Sabrina. "No." She turned toward the back entrance.

"Why not?" Sabrina pleaded.

Barbara sighed. "Because you are too valuable, where they have served their purpose. Now hurry along before your heroes arrive to pretend to save you."

"Heroes?" Sabrina murmured.

Barbara shook her head at how clueless her stepdaughter was. However, before she voiced her opinion, a rush of gentlemen forced their way into the front and back of the shoppe, surrounding Barbara and her guards. She stepped forward and pulled Sabrina into her clutches. The girl was her only chance at escaping unscathed.

"Yes, as I stated, heroes."

Sabrina looked to the front entrance and saw Graham rushing in with Lord Ralston and Lord Kincaid. DeVille strode through the back entrance with a menacing, arrogant expression. Her white knight charged to her side, followed by her black knight. They both only held her best interest at heart but for different reasons.

Her nightmare had taken a new twist.

Chapter Twenty

WITH THE ARRIVAL OF Worth and DeVille, Sabrina had failed to notice Barbara held a gun pointed to her side in warning, not as a threat to her life.

Oh, she had learned of Barbara's plan to kill her, but her stepmother had something more diabolical planned for that occasion. No. This was a warning to stay next to her or she would shoot one of her heroes. Barbara wouldn't care which one she killed. She would find enjoyment with either. Worth because he gave Sabrina hope and Barbara believed he had caused her betrayal. DeVille because of how he cared more for Sabrina than he did for Barbara, a betrayal of the highest regard for Barbara Langdale.

Lady L greeted them. "Welcome, gentlemen. I would say your presence is a surprise. However, we know it isn't."

Worth stepped forward, grasping Sabrina's hands. "Come, Sabrina, you are safe now."

Sabrina shook her head, twisting her hands out of his grasp. Panic rose in her, preventing her from speaking. She feared for Worth's life more than DeVille's. If Barbara killed Worth, she could still seek her revenge against the Worthingtons and destroy Sabrina in the process. Her expression pleaded with Worth to back away. However, he defied her wishes and grabbed her shoulders, pulling her towards him.

Barbara raised her gun to Worth's head. "What my daughter cannot say is that she remains under my control. Now please step back, Mr. Worthington, while I make my demands. If not, then you shall meet your untimely death."

"So be it," Worth snarled. "If it removes Sabrina from your clutches, then it is a sacrifice I am willing to make. You only get to pull the trigger once before you meet your demise right alongside mine."

"No," Sabrina cried. "Please, Worth, I am not worth your life. Step back and allow Barbara to make her escape."

"No!" Worth growled.

Sabrina swung her gaze to DeVille. "Please pull him away. I beg of you to help me. Make him see reason."

DeVille smiled at her with patience. "Ah, love, I wish I could grant you your request. But the gentleman is acting no different from how I would. He only stepped forward before I did."

"Please," Sabrina pleaded with DeVille.

Lady L laughed. "She still has you twisted with her innocence. I should have known you would try to play the gallant hero along with her other admirer."

DeVille bowed. "Whenever Lady Sabrina needs my help, I am but her humble servant."

"But, dear brother, she is no longer an innocent virgin," Lady L taunted. "She has spread her thighs for the man beside you. Liberties that she has always denied you, she allowed him to take."

DeVille shrugged with indifference. "It is to be expected. She loves the bloke."

Lady L scoffed. "She no longer remains pure. Do you still wish for her tarnished pussy in your bed?"

DeVille smiled at Sabrina with adoration. "I will accept Lady Sabrina however she wishes when she comes to me. She is worthy enough of any man's devotion. Especially mine."

"Hell will freeze over before I ever allow you to touch Sabrina," Worth threatened.

Lady L cackled. "You are in bed with the devil. He can make anything happen."

DeVille stepped forward and pulled Worth away from Sabrina and Lady Langdale. Worth shook his grip away and stepped back, but DeVille was no match for Worth. He stepped behind Worth and wrapped his arm around Worth's neck to hold him in place. When Worth's men moved to help him, DeVille's men moved into place around their boss.

This only brought forth more amusement for Lady Langdale, who laughed at the display of possessiveness. "Ah, two men fighting for your attention. Who will be the winner? The knight who holds your heart and fights for justice. Or the devil who wants your soul and seeks revenge? Either one, I believe you will never find boredom between the bedsheets. I am curious, daughter, on which one you will choose?"

"Unhand me, DeVille," Worth snarled.

DeVille tightened his grip in warning. "Only if you promise to keep your distance. Sabrina made a request, and you must honor her wishes." Then he whispered for only Worth to hear, "Quit reacting with your damn heart and apply your strategic reasonings to this situation."

Worth nodded, and DeVille released his hold. Worth rubbed at his neck and glared at DeVille. When he signed a deal with the devil, he had never realized that the devil held feelings for Sabrina. Now he understood why DeVille had agreed so readily to help them with this cause. He hoped to win Sabrina's affections for himself.

Worth stared at Sabrina, wondering what her feelings were for the devil. The way she pleaded with the man bothered him. They held a connection with one another that confused Worth. Who was DeVille to Sabrina? Then he remembered how Lady Langdale referred to him.

"Brother? Lady Langdale is your sister?" Worth accused.

"You didn't realize our family connection when you signed your soul away? For shame, Mr. Worthington. And you call yourself an investigator," Lady Langdale taunted Worth.

"Is this where you double-cross me?" Worth questioned DeVille.

DeVille sighed. "No. This is where Barbara plays us against each other. She is attempting to place doubt because she knows which strings to pull to make you dance. So far you are playing to her advantage. Now pull your head out of your arse and let's continue with our plan."

Worth had two options. He could either walk away from his deal with DeVille and rescue Sabrina on his own, which would end in his death. But at least she would be alive and free from Barbara Langdale. His family and friends would see to her welfare. Sabrina would never be forgotten again.

Or he could place his trust with the devil and hope Sabrina walked away unscathed. If he sided with DeVille, then the gentleman would end the torment his family had suffered the past year.

If he was honest with himself, he only had one option. He wanted a lifetime with Sabrina. He wanted a family with her. Worth wanted to love Sabrina for an eternity.

He held his hand to DeVille to reaffirm his decision. A deal with the devil to spend a lifetime with an angel was worth it. Even if his angel was really a siren who held his heart within her soul.

DeVille shook his hand and muttered lowly, "You will follow my lead."

Worth gritted his teeth but nodded. Let the bastard think what he wanted. If there was an opportunity, Worth would grab it. He hadn't made the sacrifices he had not to claim victory if a chance presented itself. Nor would he allow harm to come upon Sabrina.

DeVille faced his sister and Sabrina. He allowed his gaze to travel the length of Sabrina. She was a beauty like no other. It was a shame Barbara used her as bait, but he expected nothing less from his sister. He smiled at the jewels decorating Sabrina's dress. His sister was as devious as ever. Not only that, but he had a mole in his organization, one he would deal with later.

"You look quite lovely, Sabrina. The jewels decorating your gown make you sparkle," DeVille complimented Sabrina.

"Thank you, DeVille. However, I cannot claim credit. Barbara chose the gown and instructed the seamstress to sew on the jewels." Sabrina frowned. "I do not believe they are real."

DeVille chuckled. "Oh, they are very real, my love."

When Worth growled, Sabrina frowned and pleaded. "Please refrain from the endearments, DeVille. You are angering Worth."

"Ah, but a little healthy competition will keep the bloke in line," DeVille baited Worth.

Sabrina pinched her lips. "Please."

"Very well."

Their exchange only added to Worth's irritation. Once again Sabrina pleaded, and the devil agreed to her demands. He didn't understand why DeVille dragged out the confrontation. He wouldn't feel settled until Sabrina was out of harm's way. However, Worth must continue with his blind faith. Sabrina appeared to trust DeVille, and so must he.

"I thought you would like that added touch," Lady L said.

"Very clever of you. Taunt me with what is mine in more ways than one."

"Did you tell him?" Lady L nodded her head toward Worth.

"Our agreement was a need-to-know basis. I didn't feel he needed to know the details," DeVille responded.

"What details?" Worth questioned.

"'Tis nothing important, Worth," Sabrina whispered.

Lady L laughed again. "Do you hear that, DeVille? Sabrina said you were nothing important. So sad, little brother. It appears she favors the toff."

DeVille smiled. "I know differently how Sabrina cares for me." He waved his hand in the air. "Now enough of your attempt to cause a jealous rift between Worth and I. State your demands so we may continue with our day."

Lady Langdale pouted. "My demand is simple. Everyone will step aside while Sabrina and I make our escape. Then whatever you decide after our departure is entirely up to you. I will need one of my guards for a carriage driver, though."

"And if we do not accept your demand?" DeVille questioned.

"Then Sabrina shall meet her demise." Lady L shrugged. "Either way, it doesn't matter, for she will meet it either way. Only, if she leaves with me, it guarantees my safety."

DeVille pondered her request for only a moment before he stepped aside, signaling his guards to do the same. He waved out his hand for her to leave. "Safe journey."

"Are you mad?" Worth demanded.

Lady Langdale smirked, dragging Sabrina along with her. Sabrina glanced over her shoulder at Worth, pleading with him to save her. Worth started after them, but DeVille held him back. Her stepmother pushed her forward to escape while given the chance.

"Sabrina!" Worth yelled.

Her pleading glance tore his soul apart. It held desperation and fear, along with disappointment that he had abandoned her. He fought against DeVille's hold, struggling to free himself so he could get to her. However, it wasn't only DeVille keeping him from Sabrina. His own friends blocked his path by standing in a line to prevent him from chasing after her. It wasn't until the carriage rode past the door that DeVille relinquished his hold. But his trusted confidants remained in their vigil to block him from reaching Sabrina.

They betrayed him as he had betrayed Sabrina. He had sworn his loyalty to her, and in the end, he had failed her. He stalked away, running his hands through his hair. Worth wanted to pummel every person in this shoppe. Starting with DeVille. He tore off his suit coat and rolled up his sleeves.

That only made the bastard smirk. "We don't have time for this, Mr. Worthington. After we rescue Sabrina, if you still wish to take a shot at me, you may try."

Worth sneered. "Why in the hell did you allow her to leave?"

Ralston stepped forward to make him understand. "Because if he didn't, then Sabrina would be dead. He made the logical decision. Now focus. Where would they have gone?"

Worth closed his eyes, trying to bring himself under control. No matter how hard he tried, he struggled. He wanted to rage at everyone and express his fury, but he needed to calm down. He must focus. Sabrina's life depended on him.

"The Fitzgeralds' shoppe."

DeVille grabbed his arm. "Let's go. We can take my carriage. Everyone else spread the men around to every road leading out of town and near the docks. Just in case she has a boat ready to depart. Whatever the situation is, Sabrina's safety is our number one concern. No one is to jeopardize her life. Am I clear on this?"

Everyone murmured their agreement and took off to follow his demands. DeVille strode out of the shoppe, and Worth followed. He had no other choice if he wanted to reach Sabrina in time. They climbed into the carriage after DeVille gave his driver instructions.

As the carriage took off at a maddening pace, Worth sat with his elbows resting on his knees and his head hanging down. The carriage jerked him forward, but he caught himself before he sprawled onto the floor. He sat back in the seat and regarded the man across from him, who stared back with his eyebrow arched, waiting for Worth's fury.

"I don't know whether to thank you or slug you," Worth muttered.

"I understand your frustration. You wish to play the gallant hero, rescuing the damsel in distress, but I keep getting in your way. Then there is the matter of how twisted you are concerning Sabrina. You cannot make rational decisions because your heart is overruling your mind."

Worth sighed, staring out the window. "Nothing can happen to her."

"And nothing will," DeVille assured him.

Worth smirked. "Even the devil cannot guarantee that promise."

"Ahh, but this devil can ensure Sabrina's fate."

"What is she to you?" Worth asked.

A ghost of a smile flitted over DeVille's lips. "A promise."

Worth frowned. DeVille's answer made no sense. The man's expression stated how he didn't plan to elaborate, either.

"Thank you," Worth stated instead of questioning him further. The decision DeVille made had saved Sabrina and allowed them more time to help her. For that, he would give the man his gratitude.

DeVille nodded his acceptance. "Do you have a plan for when we reach the Fitzgeralds?"

"Yes."

DeVille waited, but the toff never said another word. It would appear Worth would get to play the white knight after all. He only hoped the man rescued the damsel in time. If not, then he would become a wreck of a man without the lovely Sabrina in his life. He had seen men like Graham Worthington before. They fell hopelessly in love and then fell apart when they lost the love of their life, turning them into lost souls, wandering through life in a state of depression nobody could lift. This bloke was already one step on his journey. It was why DeVille never allowed a soul close to his heart.

Love was a wasted emotion that sucked away one's soul.

Chapter Twenty-One

S ABRINA SAT TIED TO the chair next to the Fitzgeralds, watching her stepmother pace around the clustered shoppe. Barbara was in a state of fury, fuming over how Sabrina had ruined her plans for revenge. She blamed Sabrina for betraying her for Graham Worthington's cause. She could've destroyed the Worthingtons if Sabrina hadn't indulged in her fascination with Graham. Now only two guards remained to protect Barbara. She had lost everyone else to her failed plans. The Worthingtons had thwarted Barbara's every attempt to seek her revenge since they arrived in London.

Sabrina would rejoice at her downfall if she didn't worry about her and the Fitzgeralds' lives. Barbara was more unstable than ever, and Sabrina was unsure how she would react since they had trapped her. Barbara had watched the windows since their arrival. She paced up and down the aisles when more men arrived to capture her. Her stepmother counted them as they arrived. But throughout her mutterings, she never once mentioned if Graham or DeVille were among those numbers, which meant they weren't. Because Barbara would take pleasure if so. She would use Sabrina to taunt them.

However, she ignored Sabrina as if she had forgotten about her in her attempt to escape her ultimate downfall. Sabrina had prayed for this day to come. Now that it had arrived, she didn't feel a sense of satisfaction like she thought she would. Instead, she only held disappointment. The lady wouldn't meet the justice Sabrina had wished for. No. The lady would only meet her death today. By whose hand, Sabrina held no clue. There was no means of escape for the trap Barbara Langdale had set for herself.

Sabrina hung her head, fighting back tears. When she walked out of the tea shoppe, she had placed her faith in Graham that he would protect her. However, she had never placed her trust in him. She had kept secrets from him that affected how he reacted when under pressure. She didn't fault him for not rescuing her from Barbara's clutches when she was the one who had placed the obstacles in the path all along.

He came to her yesterday and confessed the sacrifices he made for her. Instead of being honest with him, she had allowed her fear of not trusting another soul to keep her from telling him about DeVille. After Dracott abandoned her, she'd sworn to herself that she would trust no one ever again. When Graham shouted her name as Barbara dragged her away, it had broken her heart in two. His stare had been filled with regret, anguish, and most of all, failure. He thought he had failed her when it was Sabrina who had failed him.

"Have faith, my dear. He will come for you," Mrs. Fitzgerald whispered.

Sabrina raised her head and attempted a smile. "I fear he is too late. I am sorry."

The tears Sabrina tried to hold back streamed down her face. The Fitzgeralds were the kindest souls Sabrina had ever had the fortune to meet. They had taken her under their wing and offered her comfort from Barbara Langdale's cruelty. In return, Sabrina had helped them with her limited funds. But it wasn't enough. Now they sat tied up because she showed how she cared for them. Barbara Langdale hurt everyone she had ever cared for. For years, it had been Dracott. Now she would destroy Graham before she met her demise.

Barbara Langdale waited for Graham to arrive before she killed Sabrina. She wanted Graham to watch so her death would torment him for the rest of his life. While Mrs. Fitzgerald believed he would show, Sabrina prayed he wouldn't. But her heart cried how he would.

"Where is your knight, Sabrina?" Barbara taunted.

Sabrina glared at Barbara. "Why did you kill my father?"

Barbara sighed, rolling her eyes. "You know why, my dear."

Sabrina cringed at the fake endearment. "Because he had the evidence to persecute you."

Barbara waved her hand in the air as if it was inconsequential. "None of that mattered. He betrayed me by marrying me under false pretenses. For that reason alone, I had your father murdered. Well, that and he had served his purpose. I hungered for more excitement and he stood in the way."

"Why not leave?"

"I told you. He betrayed me. I allow no one to double-cross me without seeking my revenge. As you will learn here shortly."

"He will kill you," Sabrina threatened.

Barbara sneered. "Yes. But not before I kill you and watch him weep."

A commotion sounded near the back entrance, and Barbara signaled her guard to check it out. Sabrina tensed, expecting Graham to appear.

However, the guard came back, shrugging his shoulder. "Just a dog and cat fighting, knocking over some crates."

"What is taking him so long? If he doesn't arrive soon, we will just set the place on fire before we steal away. While I would rather enjoy watching his sorrow, I need to protect myself. We must escape, and the fire will be the distraction we need," Barbara explained her strategy.

Barbara and her guards moved to the windows and whispered about the rest of their plans. They faced the front of the store. Sabrina wondered if she could get the Fitzgeralds to safety.

When someone ran past the opening and pressed against the wall, Sabrina gasped and turned to see if Barbara saw them, but her stepmother remained focused on herself. Sabrina saw another figure sneak in and prayed it wasn't Graham.

When Dracott stuck his head out, her fear increased. Barbara would take as much pleasure in hurting Dracott as she would Graham. Dracott had been her protector for years, irritating Barbara each time he welcomed Sabrina's punishment. Dracott held a finger over his lips and winked at her before ducking behind the counter.

Sabrina focused her attention on Barbara to issue a warning to Dracott if needed. However, it was never necessary because Barbara never abandoned her vigil at the windows. Dracott snuck around to them.

"You are a fool," Sabrina whispered.

"You left me with no other choice, my friend," Dracott drawled.

"Hurry, help the Fitzgeralds to safety," Sabrina ordered.

"And you, too."

Sabrina shook her head. "No. Not until I know they are safe."

"Graham gave me an order to ignore your stubbornness." Dracott sliced a knife through her bindings.

Sabrina grabbed his hands. "He is not here, is he?"

Dracott shook his head at her with a smile. "Now why would he stay away?"

Sabrina whipped her head toward the back entrance as Graham strolled into the shoppe, followed by a group of gentlemen. She stared at Ravencroft in disbelief. Dracott's brother had disliked her from the start, and now he was here to help save her. Graham never looked at her once. His only focus was on Lady Langdale.

"Now, Dracott!" Graham ordered.

Dracott guided the Fitzgeralds out of danger, tugging Sabrina behind them. However, Sabrina maneuvered her way out of his grip and ran toward Graham.

"Get her out of here!" Graham shouted.

"Graham, come with me," Sabrina pleaded.

Graham still wouldn't look at Sabrina. He avoided her plea and continued toward Lady Langdale. Ravencroft gathered Sabrina in his arms and tried to lead her away, but she scratched and clawed at him, resisting his hold. However, he was no match for her and removed her from the shoppe.

She pounded her fists against his chest. "I hate you," she cried.

"I know you do, Sabrina. And you have every right to. My treatment of you in the past has been deplorable. However, my actions today are in your best interest," Ravencroft said.

"Why?" Tears streamed down Sabrina's cheeks. She needed to protect Graham and Ravencroft prevented her from saving him.

"Because Graham needs to focus when he confronts Lady Langdale and he cannot when he worries about you. You are a distraction that will bring him to harm. Can you not see how much you mean to him?" Ravencroft explained.

"She will kill him."

"Have faith in Graham. He holds it for you."

"What is his plan?" Sabrina asked.

Dracott answered her from behind. "For you to wait outside while he ends Lady Langdale's reign of terror."

Ravencroft dropped his hold and turned her into Dracott's arms. Dracott wrapped her in his embrace and held her while she cried out her fear for Graham. "The Fitzgeralds?"

"They are safe," Dracott assured her.

"Will you please let me go?"

"No, I cannot. An order from Graham. You are to remain in our hold until he holds you for himself."

Sabrina stomped on his foot. "You are unfair."

Dracott groaned. "And you are a terror I'll do anything to protect."

Another argument rested on the tip of Sabrina's tongue when the sound of a gunshot ripped through the air. Her eyes widened, and she gripped Dracott. Her gaze pleaded for him to reassure her of Graham's safety. However, his gaze only held the same worry and doubt as hers. When her knees buckled, he swept her in his arms and carried her to the side of the building. He slid down with her on his lap and rocked her quivering body.

"Shh, love." Dracott didn't know how to console Sabrina when he was unsure what had happened. Graham had yet to show himself to reassure them he lived. Fear for Graham's life gripped him when no one rushed out. He shot a look to his brother, and Ravencroft ran off to enter the building.

Sabrina's tears tore Dracott apart. If anything happened to Graham, it would destroy her. She had suffered so much and deserved a lifetime of happiness. It was within her grasp, but like always, Barbara Langdale stole it away from Sabrina. In her spiteful regard to torment Sabrina, she had set a path of destruction for today. Now it played out to its end.

Dracott prayed it was to Sabrina's advantage.

Barbara Langdale strolled along the aisle with her usual arrogance. Her guards followed closely behind. "Welcome back, Mr. Worthington. It appears you lost a fellow knight. Did you not care for the competition?" Lady L taunted.

"DeVille is no competition," Worth drawled.

"Ah, you could not be more mistaken. Sabrina and DeVille share a questionable past with one another. In my opinion, it should've been you who helped her to escape, not Dracott. Another fool my daughter captivated to do her bidding. She has a tendency to collect them wherever we land."

Worth leaned against the counter in casual disregard while Lady Langdale attempted to slander Sabrina's virtue. They were all lies. However, he allowed the lady to ramble because it allowed DeVille to get into position. Whatever the relationship between Sabrina and DeVille, it was a moment in her past. As for Dracott, he and Sabrina held a friendship most would envy. Either would make sacrifices for the other because they loved one another as a brother and sister.

"It does not matter to me about Sabrina's past. As for DeVille, he has been a formidable ally today. Tell me, how do you feel now that your reign of terror is over? Have you become desperate yet? Any last-minute ploys up your sleeve?" Worth mocked her.

"I am far from over," Lady L snarled.

Worth spun in a circle. "Look around you. We have surrounded the place and only two guards remain to protect you. And from the looks of them, they want to flee."

"They are my most loyal servants and would never abandon me," Lady L gloated.

"Shall we see?" Worth asked.

He wanted her left standing all alone when he destroyed her. To show her how no one pledged their loyalty out of their own free will. He wanted her as defenseless as Sabrina had been since her father died. To quiver in fear all alone while they sought their justice. He wouldn't kill her. No, he refused to tarnish his hands with her blood. DeVille was more than welcome to seek his justice in that form. Worth only wanted to seek the vindication of his years chasing her to an end. But most of all, he wanted vindication for Sabrina. She deserved no less.

As much as he wanted to gather her in his arms and carry her from this hell, he resisted and never glanced in her direction. If he did, he would've crumbled at her despair. Also, he was a coward. He couldn't bear to see the disappointment in her gaze again. It was what kept him to continue with this farce. He would prove he was worthy of her love by destroying her greatest fear.

"Gentlemen, you may leave of your own free will. I guarantee your safety if you leave Lady Langdale's service," Worth lied. DeVille's men waited for them.

Lady L laughed at his feeble attempt. However, her laughter faded away when both guards backed away from her. She turned toward them. "Do not take one more step," she ordered.

They stopped, glancing over her shoulder at Worth. He shrugged as if he didn't care what decision they made. He didn't think they were too addle-witted not to realize the dire consequences they were under. However, he'd witnessed other circumstances where people regretted not making the wise decision. It didn't take them long to run out the door.

"Lady Langdale left all alone. What a shame." He glanced over to his brother and friends who stood by his side. "Not really. Quite glorious from where I stand."

"Gloat all you want, Mr. Worthington. Because your time has come to an end too." Lady Langdale aimed her pistol at him and pulled the trigger.

When he heard the cock of her pistol, Worth turned back toward Lady Langdale and prepared himself for the shot, but DeVille rushed in and knocked Lady L's arm upwards. The bullet hit the ceiling, knocking the tiles loose around them.

"It took you long enough," Worth muttered.

"My apologies, Mr. Worthington. My delay was to allow you time to rescue the damsel in distress. Is Sabrina safe?" DeVille asked.

Lady L scoffed. "He didn't rescue her. He gave the honor to Dracott."

DeVille nodded. "A worthy hero."

"I thought so," Worth commented.

DeVille gripped Lady Langdale's wrist. "Are you finished with her?"

"Yes, I believe I am. I have realized I no longer desire to listen to her lies and I'm ready to close this chapter in my life. You are more than welcome to her," Worth stated.

When Lady Langdale threw out her taunts about Sabrina, Worth had realized that anything she uttered from her mouth would be a lie. They could question her for endless hours, and the result would be the same. They would never understand her reasons for wreaking havoc on innocent victims, other than a streak of diabolical madness ran through her veins. In his quest to bring her to justice, he had forgotten why he began the search for her. To rid society of her evilness and give her victims peace of mind. In his search, he had discovered Sabrina, and his priorities had changed. He no longer needed to seek his revenge against a person unworthy of his emotions, not when he needed to cherish the lady who had suffered from the injustice of Barbara Langdale's reign of terror. Sabrina.

He walked away without another glance. He never wanted to set eyes on the lady again. She had fallen. While he held pride in the victory, his only concern was for Sabrina.

Worth stepped out of the building to find Sabrina clinging to Dracott in misery. He hurried to their side and lifted her into his arms. "Shh, my love. No more tears, only smiles from your siren's lips," Worth teased.

Sabrina lifted her head at his voice. "Graham?"

Worth pressed a kiss to her lips. "Yes."

"I thought she shot you," Sabrina cried.

"She tried." At Sabrina's gasp, he cringed. It was a detail he should've kept from her. But he didn't want any secrets between them.

She cupped his cheek. His soft bristles were forming again. She loved him so much. He was her gallant hero, her white knight, the love of her life. He was every dream come true. However, she didn't deserve him yet. Not until she fulfilled her obligations. Worth wouldn't understand the circumstances about to happen. He would see it as a sign of betrayal. If the depth of their love was as strong as Sabrina imagined, then when she returned, he would accept her with open arms. And if he didn't, then their love was only a figment of her imagination.

"I love you with all my heart and soul, Graham Worthington. I only hope you will forgive me," Sabrina whispered before pressing her lips against his.

"I love you, Sabrina." The regret in her gaze confused him. "What is there to forgive?"

DeVille came to stand near them. "Sabrina?"

Worth glanced at DeVille, who was holding his hand out for Sabrina. "What is this?"

"Please set me down, Graham," Sabrina said.

Worth shook his head. "No. You were never part of the deal."

"You remember, Mr. Worthington, when you asked what my payment was, and I informed you I would ask a favor in return? This is my favor. Please release Sabrina into my care."

"Never," Worth snarled.

DeVille had realized this would happen and only hoped Sabrina could convince Worth to release her before he had to use force. He hated to hurt the gentleman over a simple misunderstanding.

"Graham, I must leave with DeVille. Please," Sabrina pleaded.

Instead of her pleading with DeVille, she now pleaded with Worth to relinquish his hold. Sabrina appeared willing to leave with DeVille. None of this made sense to him. What made it more confusing was how Sabrina never offered an explanation. She expected him to release her and allow her to walk away from him. Never.

"Please. I cannot stand to watch you come to any harm. Do not make me watch such a travesty. I cannot handle any more trauma today." Sabrina's quiet plea left Worth with no other option but to release her into DeVille's possession.

He slid Sabrina along his body but didn't release his hold. Instead, he brought her flush against him and devoured her lips her with a desperation unknown to him. He felt his soul departing from him with her abandonment. Worth pulled kiss after kiss from her lips, drowning in her hold. She clung to him and returned his affection with her own desperation. He tasted their despair with each swipe of their tongues battling for survival.

Sabrina's tears flowed as she lost herself in Graham's anguish. He thought she meant to leave him forever and ravished her lips, staking his claim before he released her to DeVille. She tried to soothe him with her kisses but failed.

They only turned more desperate. She wanted to confess the last of her secrets, but she must return with DeVille first.

Sabrina pulled away, pressing her forehead against his. "You are the only soul who has ever held my heart. Do not lose your hold."

Sabrina pressed one more kiss upon his lips before she joined her hand with DeVille's. She never glanced back once.

She feared he'd hand her heart back.

Chapter Twenty-Two

S ABRINA SLIPPED INTO HER bedchamber at DeVille's home, drawing off her shawl. The evenings had turned cooler, with each autumn day slipping away. Before long, the crisp winter air would linger, stealing away her chance to watch Graham from afar. Already this evening, the rain had stolen her opportunity away. Graham had returned to his bedchamber after his usual ritual of a cigar and a drink of whiskey. She wondered if his nightmares still plagued him or if he had recovered.

"When will you end the bloke's torment?" DeVille asked.

Sabrina jumped, letting out a screech. Her hand clutched at her heart as she watched DeVille light the candle next to him. "Must you frighten me?"

"My apologies, my lady," DeVille mocked.

Sabrina growled at him. She should've expected that he waited for her return. He had visited every night since she started sneaking out. DeVille had warned her of the danger and pleaded with her to talk to Graham instead of sneaking around in the dark of night to watch him from afar. He didn't understand what prevented Sabrina from sharing her secrets with Graham. She didn't understand it herself, only that at her every attempt, she allowed her doubt to keep her silent.

She curled up on the divan, waiting for his lecture. Sabrina enjoyed their discussions. It helped to keep her panic attacks at bay. Since her freedom from Barbara Langdale, life had overwhelmed her more than it had while in her clutches. At times, she didn't know how to cope, but DeVille talked her through it. His guidance had been salvation for her soul. She owed DeVille her sanity.

Sabrina frowned over his silence. "No lecture this evening?"

DeVille stared at her. "No, my dear."

"Why not?"

"Because they only fall on deaf ears. You do not heed my advice but continue to make yourself suffer."

Sabrina picked at the strings on her shawl. "I am afraid."

DeVille sat forward. "Of what?"

"He will not forgive me."

DeVille clasped his hands in front of him. "The man searches for you everywhere. Every day he returns to the same haunts and walks away in despair. Graham Worthington is eager to welcome you with open arms. Why would he not forgive you?"

Sabrina bit at her bottom lip. "Because I left willingly with you."

DeVille shook his head. "No. You will not guilt me over this. I needed to fulfill an obligation, and you promised me I could whenever you were free from Barbara."

Sabrina sighed. "I know. I'm sorry."

DeVille nodded his acceptance of her apology. "He will forgive you. The bloke is hopelessly in love with you."

Sabrina giggled. "You say that as if it is a tragic event."

DeVille smiled. "It is good to hear you laugh."

Sabrina took on a pinched expression again. She felt guilty for enjoying her time with DeVille when Graham wandered around in misery. However, she couldn't return to him until her soul had healed. Her stay with DeVille had been a good start. She didn't want Graham to see her as a victim but as a survivor. She refused to start their life with the wounds of her past between them.

What Sabrina wanted might be impossible to receive. She wanted to begin her journey living as a lady, not a heathen. She wanted Graham to court her with his undying devotion. Sabrina wanted to fulfill every fantasy she had held as a girl and every fantasy she held now as a woman.

"It is time for me to leave," Sabrina whispered.

DeVille moved to sit next to Sabrina and pulled her into his arms. "I know. Colebourne will have a carriage waiting for you in the morning. Thank you for allowing me to care for you this past month."

Sabrina sniffed, wiping away a tear. "You will hold my gratitude forever for helping me heal."

DeVille tipped her chin up. "It has been an honor, my lady."

He rose after pressing a kiss to her forehead. Sabrina watched DeVille walk away.

"Wait," she called out. Sabrina ran to the nightstand and pulled out a small bag. DeVille stepped forward, and Sabrina pressed the bag into his hand. "These are yours."

DeVille opened the bag and spread the contents into his palm. The emeralds glittered from the firelight. He smiled, poured them back into the bag, and handed it back to Sabrina. "No, my dear. They are yours."

"But . . ."

DeVille pressed his finger against her lip. "Your father offered those as payment to protect you, and I failed. When I gave them to Barbara, they were to be in exchange for your hand. But my sister double-crossed me and kept you and the jewels. Consider them my gift for you as you begin your new journey."

"But . . ."

"But nothing. Consider them a wedding present." DeVille winked at her and walked away.

He wouldn't see her off in the morning. This was his goodbye. DeVille would relinquish his obligation toward her to Colebourne, another gentleman who wanted to fulfill a promise from her father. All these years, Sabrina had thought of herself alone, but her father had secured her protection before his death. However, she had resisted the protection to seek vengeance for his death. While she never achieved her vengeance, she had filled her heart with the love surrounding her.

Now she only needed the courage to approach her love.

The soft sprinkles of raindrops fell on Graham as he nursed his glass of whiskey on the terrace outside his bedchamber. Another nightmare had dragged him from his bed. The same one ran in loops every time he drifted to sleep. The only difference was he had a name to shout, but like before, she only gazed at him with her despair before she floated away.

He set the glass and cigar down and rubbed at the bristles on his face. They ached for Sabrina's soft caress. Each day without her broke his heart into another chunk. He feared it would crumble into dust soon. He waited for her return, but she continued to deny them their happiness.

In his agony, he never blamed her for her abandonment. However, he was slowly losing patience in waiting for her to come to him. Even though he had searched for her everywhere and she continued to elude him, he had sensed her presence. She was nearby but, once again, forever out of his reach. He just wished to understand why she stayed away.

Every day he visited every spot they had shared a moment together. His family even helped by attending every function they received invitations to in hopes she would attend. They wanted to welcome Sabrina into their family embrace. However, no one had seen her. Graham had stormed DeVille's club every day, but his guards refused him entry. He wanted an explanation, but none was forthcoming. He planned one more attempt tomorrow.

The sky started pelting him with its fury after it finished teasing him with gentle raindrops. He understood its despair, for it wrapped Graham in its warm embrace and kept him smothered. Graham wrapped the blanket around him tighter and lifted his head to the sky. He welcomed the misery into his soul; it kept him grounded. Because tomorrow the sun would shine and give him the hope he needed. He refused to allow life to defeat him.

Before long, he would kiss his siren's lips once again.

Sabrina finished unpacking her few belongings. She only had a few dresses in her possession because DeVille had insisted on purchasing them for her. And she couldn't very well continue to wear the green dress Barbara bought. It held too many horrible memories for her. She had burned it after she plucked the emeralds from the dress. She moved to the vanity and traced the roses on the ribbon Graham had gifted her with.

Sabrina missed Graham and longed for his arms to wrap her in his warm embrace. She noticed when spying how he had grown his beard again. *Was it for her?* She ached to feel the bristles scraping across her skin. *Did he miss her, too?* Sabrina only had to see him to find out. *Why did she make them suffer?*

Sabrina turned at the knock on the open door and saw Colebourne.

"Have you settled, my dear?"

Sabrina smiled. "Yes."

Colebourne held out his hand. "May I come in?"

Sabrina nodded, moving to sit in a chair by the fireplace. "Thank you for offering me a place to stay."

Colebourne settled into a chair. "It is my privilege to welcome you into my home for as long as you need."

"I do not mean to be a burden."

Colebourne chuckled. "You are no burden. I welcome the company. Lucas and Abigail never leave Colebourne Manor. My townhome only fills when my family visits for tea. In which case, Evelyn is due any moment. Would you like to join us?"

Hope blossomed in Sabrina, but she swiftly tampered it down. It wouldn't be fair to Graham if she visited with his family before him. She owed him her attention before anyone else. "Not on this visit." When Colebourne appeared upset with her answer, she reassured him, "But soon."

Colebourne nodded. "Very well then. I've instructed my staff not to inform anyone about your visit. So your secret is safe until you change your mind. I will keep Evelyn occupied so she does not wander."

Sabrina frowned. "Is there a reason she wouldn't stay in the parlor?"

Colebourne chuckled. "As revenge for my matchmaking, my family likes to cause chaos and leave pranks to keep me on my toes."

Sabrina smiled as he described his family with fondness. She wondered how different it would be to live amongst a boisterous family. She sensed Graham's family acted in the same manner as Colebourne's. "They sound lovely."

"They are, my dear. So are the Worthingtons. Especially Graham."

"I've heard of your tales of matchmaking, and I forbid it."

Colebourne winked at her. "That is the beauty of matchmaking, my dear. It happens when you least expect it."

Sabrina shook her head at him as he left her alone with her thoughts. She needed to prepare herself for Graham. Because Colebourne wouldn't let her wallow in doubt as DeVille had. DeVille only had because of his guilty conscience. However, Sabrina sensed the duke had never held guilt over anything, least of all past mistakes and ones that kept him from making his point.

Sabrina sensed her stay would result in the duke's matchmaking attempt.

Instead of storming DeVille's office the next morning, Worth acted as a gentleman and requested a meeting. His gracious approach earned him an open door, followed by DeVille offering him a drink.

Worth settled in a chair in front of DeVille's desk. "No, thank you. I only wish to see Sabrina."

DeVille steepled his fingers together. "I am sorry, mate. She is no longer under my care."

Worth sat forward in his chair. "Where has she gone?"

"That I am not at the liberty to say. I promised her my silence."

Worth slammed his fists on DeVille's desk and drew the guards' attention. DeVille waved them away, allowing Worth his frustration. He rose and poured the gentleman a drink, even though he had refused one. They needed to discuss the events leading to Sabrina's absence.

"Take this." DeVille thrust the glass in Worth's hand.

Worth threw the whiskey back and grimaced at the burn. "I don't understand."

"That is Sabrina for you. She twists you in knots until you are helpless."

"You care for her," Worth mumbled.

"Yes. But not in the way you think." DeVille decided to put the bloke out of his misery. It was the least he could do since Sabrina refused to. DeVille relaxed back in his chair. "I made a promise to her father, and I failed to protect her. When Langdale married my sister, I warned him of her. But he refused to listen. Then I learned how he had gathered evidence of Barbara's crimes. He denied my requests for protection but made me promise to help Sabrina if something should happen to him. However, Barbara slipped away into the night with Sabrina before I could save her."

"None of this explains why Sabrina left with you," Worth stated.

"I tracked them down on the Continent and offered my sister a trade. Throughout the process, Sabrina pleaded with me to let her stay because she was close to proving Barbara killed her father. I refused her, explaining my obligation. However, Barbara double-crossed me. When they arrived in London at the start of the season, Sabrina came to me and asked for a loan. She promised when the time came, she would allow me to fulfill my obligation," DeVille finished explaining.

"You gave her the money so she could help the Fitzgeralds."

DeVille nodded. "And countless others."

"And her debt?"

"She never had a debt. I gave her the money, asking nothing in return except for her promise."

"Where did she go?" Worth demanded.

DeVille stood and signaled to his guards that the meeting was over. "She will return to you soon, Mr. Worthington. Allow her the time she needs to conquer her fears."

Worth frowned. "What fears? She has no reason to fear me."

DeVille smiled with patience. "She fears the feelings coursing through her. Sabrina has lived an unstable life for so long, stability frightens her. She fears it will disappear again."

Worth allowed DeVille to guide him to the door. "And my debt to you?"

DeVille slapped Worth on the back. "Became fulfilled when you allowed Sabrina to come with me. However, if I ever learn of her unhappiness, I shall revoke my decision."

Worth turned to state how he would never allow Sabrina to suffer a day of unhappiness. However, DeVille slammed the door in his face. While he never discovered Sabrina's whereabouts, he came away with a sense that their time was near.

Sabrina was within his grasp once again.

After finding a book to read in the duke's small library down the hall, Sabrina walked into her bedchamber. She frowned at the wardrobe and went to close it, but she spotted a little girl running her hand over the sequins on her gown. Mrs. Fitzgerald had surprised Sabrina when she retrieved the gown for her. It was a memory she treasured from her time with Graham. The little girl clutched a rag doll in her other hand. It was like the one Graham had purchased the day she shared tea with him and his mother.

"Hello," Sabrina greeted.

The girl turned and gasped. "You are the mermaid."

Sabrina smiled. "Mermaid?"

The girl nodded. "Yes, the one my Uncle Gam is going to marry."

Sabrina stood speechless at the girl's declaration. Then the girl slipped her hand into hers, staring at her in awe. "He wants to marry me?"

"Oh yes. He told us during tea after Mrs. Potts asked if you were pretty. But he made us promise to keep a secret."

"Mrs. Potts?" It seemed Sabrina could only repeat the girl's words. Sabrina sat on the bed.

"Yes, she is another friend of mine." The girl lifted the doll, showing Sabrina how she considered the doll her friend. "My name is Mina."

"Sabrina." Graham was correct. The girl was a doll herself and in the process of winning Sabrina over.

The girl's lips puckered. "You have a pretty name. But I do not think you are pretty."

"Oh." Sabrina swept her hand along her hair. Mina's words stung.

"I agree with Uncle Gam. You are beyond lovely." Mina reached out to touch Sabrina's hair.

"Lovely?" Mina's comment crumbled the rest of Sabrina's defenses.

Mina touched the hair clip. "Uncle Gam wears one on his suit coat. He told me it is a signal to the mermaid at how much he loves her. Do you wear one to show Uncle Gam how much you love him?"

Sabrina unclipped the decoration. "Yes. Perhaps you would like to wear it?"

Mina's eyes lit up with her excitement. "Oh yes. Then Uncle Gam can see how much I love him."

Sabrina smiled. "Only if you promise not to mention my name."

Mina nodded. The mermaid attached the hair clip and led her to the mirror to admire how it shined in her hair.

"Now you are a lovely mermaid, too."

Mina beamed, swishing her hair back and forth. When she heard her mother calling her name, her eyes widened. She had promised her mama she wouldn't wander.

"Mina. Where are you, my love? It is time to return home. Papa is waiting for us," Evelyn called out.

Sabrina lowered, held a finger to her lips, and whispered, "Remember, you never met me. Now run along."

Mina kissed her cheek. "Thank you, lovely mermaid." She turned back. "Will you come visit and have tea with Mrs. Potts and me?"

"I would love to."

Mina skipped out the door.

"There you are, love. Come, say goodbye to Uncle Theo."

Sabrina ducked behind the bed in case Evelyn came near her bedchamber. She noticed Mina left her doll behind. She crossed her legs and sat with the doll on her lap, smiling over the visit she had with Mina. One brief visit and she had fallen in love with another Worthington. Would her children with Graham hold the same wonder and imagination? Sabrina might have gotten ahead of herself, considering she still stayed away. However, she believed her imagination would ring true.

After all, Graham had told Mrs. Potts he planned to marry her.

Chapter Twenty-Three

G RAHAM STOOD OUTSIDE THE breakfast room, listening to his boisterous family talking and teasing each other. Like every morning since Lady Langdale's capture, his sisters and their husbands graced the table. They wished to show their support for his sorrow. Each day, they tried to pull a laugh from him or make him smile. However, each day he found it more difficult to join them. He turned to leave, deciding to eat breakfast at his club. No sense in depressing his family again.

However, before he could sneak away, Mina came skipping toward him, with Evelyn following behind her. Mina slipped her hand into his. "Come, Uncle Gam, Mrs. Potts wants to eat breakfast with you too."

He stared down at his niece and realized he couldn't refuse her request. Not when she offered her love and acceptance so freely. Evelyn smiled at him with her usual pity and patted his arm as she walked in to join Reese at the table. He let Mina lead him along. His family grew quiet when they saw him enter but started back with their animated discussion when they saw Mina.

Graham settled Mina between Noel and Maggie before he took a seat next to Eden. His sister squeezed his arm in affection before returning to her conversation with their mother. His heart wasn't in it, but he wouldn't disappoint Mina. He watched Maggie help to position Mrs. Potts against a bowl of fruit.

"What a beautiful hair clip, Mina," Noel gushed.

Mina beamed, swishing her head back and forth for everyone to see. "Thank you."

Maggie's gaze narrowed. "It looks like the one Graham wears clipped to his pocket every day."

Graham lifted his head to look at Mina. He had paid little attention when Noel complimented her. He figured it was the usual hair clips young girls wore. However, shining from his niece's hair was the hair clip he gave Sabrina.

Evelyn glanced at Graham and noted his desperation to learn where Mina had acquired the hair clip. "Mina, honey, where did you find such a treasure?"

Mina's lips puckered as she thought of how to answer her mama. The lovely mermaid had made her promise not to say her name. But she never said she couldn't tell anyone how she met a mermaid. She picked up Mrs. Potts and whispered her problem to her friend. Then she put the doll to her ear as she listened to her friend's advice.

"Uncle Gam's mermaid gave it to me."

"Sabrina?" Graham croaked out.

Mina's eyes widened. "I promised her not to say."

Graham swung his head at Evelyn to help him. He had no clue how to rationalize with his niece on this delicate subject.

However, before Evelyn could intervene, Reese stepped in. "That was thoughtful of her. Did you enjoy meeting the mermaid?"

"Yes, Papa. But I made her sad, too."

Reese rose and picked up Mina, setting her on his lap. "I am sure you did not mean to."

"Why was she sad?" Eden asked.

"I told her she had a pretty name. But that I didn't think she was pretty." Mina picked up her scone to take a bite.

"That was not very kind, Mina," Reese reprimanded her softly.

"But then I told her I agreed with Uncle Gam how she was lovely beyond words. Then I told her how he planned to marry her." Mina gasped, covering her mouth. "Sorry, Uncle Gam. Mrs. Potts and I were supposed to keep your secret."

A chorus of ahhs echoed around the table. Reese chuckled. Yes, his brother had fallen hard. So hard he had shared secrets with his daughter and her dolls. Oh, the family would enjoy making him suffer for his unrequited love.

"That is all right, poppet. Where did you see Sabrina?" Graham reassured his niece.

Mina shook her head. "I did not say I saw Sabrina. I visited with the lovely mermaid."

Evelyn took pity on Graham. "Was the lovely mermaid at Uncle Theo's when we visited yesterday?"

Mina nodded, pouring honey over her scone. "I left my doll for her to play with since she gave me the hair clip."

"Very kind of you, love." Reese kissed Mina on the top of her head.

Mina reached up with her sticky fingers to pull her dad's head to whisper into his ear. "Do you think Uncle Gam sees how much I love him since I am wearing the hair clip? He is sad like the mermaid and I want to make him smile."

Graham rose and picked up his niece, swinging her around. Mina had just answered his prayers. "Uncle Gams sees and loves you just as much." He gave her a loud smacking kiss on the cheek.

Mina giggled. "Now put me down." She gathered Mrs. Potts from the table. "Come, Mrs. Potts, we have a guest to prepare for."

Evelyn looked at her husband in confusion.

"What guest, Mina?" Reese called out.

"Why, the mermaid. Who else?"

Her question caused everyone to laugh over her matter-of-fact innocence.

"Such a shame how Mrs. Potts learns of your marriage proposal before your own mother," Lady Worthington quipped.

Graham groaned. It would now begin. They would start their endless torment of teasing. He sat back in his chair with a grin and embraced them, one after another. His niece gave him the hope he had searched for. He knew where to find Sabrina and would claim her today.

"Do you think they will seek Mrs. Potts's advice for the wedding ceremony?" Noel teased.

"I am sure Mina and Mrs. Potts will throw them an engagement ball," Maggie added.

Eden laughed. "Graham will be the only gentleman of the ton whose front row of wedding guests is comprised of dolls."

Reese smirked. "You are forgetting one detail, dear sisters."

Graham narrowed his gaze at his brother, asking for his sisters. "What?"

"He has yet to locate her and offer his proposal. And who knows if the girl will say yes. She keeps running, and he keeps chasing." Reese laughed at his amusement of his brother falling in love.

Graham folded his arms across his chest. "Obviously, she intends for me to catch her. Why else would she give Mina the hair clip?"

"To tease you. Why else?" Reese baited him.

Evelyn reprimanded his teasing. "Reese."

"What, my love? He deserves it for all the times he tormented me."

"You deserved those. He does not. Hold some sympathy for your brother." Evelyn tried frowning at her husband, but the teasing sparkle in his eyes was hard to resist.

Reese chuckled, rising to gather Evelyn in his arms. He kissed her with his happiness at having his family settled. Evelyn melted into his arms and pulled him in closer.

"She didn't last on my side for very long," Graham quipped. "Mother, please voice your objection over their affections. It is unbearable to watch while I am trying to eat."

"Hush. Before long, you will wish to do the same with Sabrina."

Graham watched his brother and Evelyn and knew his mother was correct.

Before long.

Graham slammed the door shut to the house near his office. The day had started with a promise and ended in the same hopelessness.

After breakfast, he had rushed to Colebourne's townhome with a bouquet of flowers, eager to see Sabrina. However, Colebourne had invited him into his study and informed him how Sabrina had left after one day in his care. He didn't know where she went because she had slipped away throughout the night. She had left Colebourne a note that expressed her gratitude but informed him how she was ready to forge her own path in life. Sabrina had left no clues to where she might have disappeared to. So he had continued his day by visiting every haunt again. But like his other visits, she was nowhere to be found.

He tugged off his coat and slung it over the chair before sitting down and discarding his boots. He refused to return home without her. His family expected him to arrive with Sabrina on his arm. He knew they would hold the same disappointment in the news of her disappearance.

Graham frowned when he stared at the flowers on the tables. They reminded him of the bouquet he bought for Sabrina. He had left them at Colebourne's in his frustration at hitting another obstacle. The softness of the petals reminded him of Sabrina's silky skin. He stepped into the living room and stopped when he noticed a fire burned in the hearth.

Not only did the fire draw his attention, but the other slight changes confused him. A book lay open on the table in front of the sofa. The blanket was spread out as if someone had used it to cover themselves. When he drew closer, he saw a cup of tea rested near the book. Graham stilled when he heard something move abovestairs.

He snuck up the steps and followed the candlelight leading to his bedchamber. He was unprepared for the sight that greeted him. A single candle flickered on the nightstand. Sabrina lay in the tub with her head thrown over the rim and her eyes closed. He gripped the doorjamb, unsure how to proceed. She left him speechless once again.

"I thought I might have to lure you with my siren's call." Sabrina's husky whisper tempted him to come closer.

Sabrina drifted her fingers through the water across her chest. She never opened her eyes but knew the exact moment when Graham arrived. Her heart settled with contentment. When he never responded, she turned her head to the side and opened her eyes. Graham had moved forward without a sound and knelt before the bathtub, staring at her with wonder.

She lifted her hand and cupped his bristled cheek. Sabrina ached to feel them brushing against her thighs. "You are a pirate once again."

Graham clutched his hand over hers. He refused to let her go again. "Always for you," he croaked out.

Sabrina traced his lips, needing to see his smile. It would show he forgave her. "You are not smiling again."

"Because I thought I lost the other half of my soul."

"I am sorry," Sabrina choked out. Her fingers trembled on his lips. She had crushed him, and it broke her heart. Tears slid along her cheeks at the torment she had caused him because she feared happiness.

"Ahh, love." Graham scooped Sabrina out of the water and carried her to the bed, never releasing his hold.

He brushed the hair from her eyes, searching for answers. Her expression no longer held loss or desperation. Instead, they shined with hope and her love for him. Graham lowered his head and drew her lips between his. Sabrina's moan invaded his soul and spread its warmth throughout him. She had come home to him.

Sabrina lost herself in Graham's kiss that spoke of the love he held for her. Her pirate harbored no ill feelings for her, other than his despair at missing her. Each kiss declared how much he missed her. Sabrina tore at the buttons on his shirt, needing to feel him against her.

Graham would have chuckled at Sabrina's eagerness if his own madness to feel her soft skin caressing him didn't consume him. He ripped the shirt off, sending buttons flying everywhere. Her eager fingers tore at the placket of his trousers. His siren's impatience only stroked his desire. When she guided the trousers over his hips and slid her hand around his cock, he realized the siren had entranced him under her spell once again. He was forever at her mercy.

Graham moaned. "Sabrina."

Sabrina lifted her lashes to stare at Graham. The desire brimming in his eyes as she slid her hand along his cock astounded her. She never imagined her touch would fuel his passion to helplessness. She lowered her lips around him, her tongue licking off the dew on the tip. Graham's hands speared through her hair, holding her to him.

He held them still. "You do not have to . . ."

Sabrina didn't have to; she wanted to. She wanted to express her love for Graham in every way possible. Her mouth lowered, drawing him in deeper. Graham swore and guided her head in a rhythm to please him. Her tongue teased him with each stroke in and out of her mouth. Graham's swearing turned into incoherent mumbles. When she sucked the tip of his cock between her lips, her tongue sliced back and forth across the slit, savoring his wetness. Graham arched off the bed and drove his cock deeper into her mouth.

Graham lost himself to the passion with each lick of her tongue. He was on the verge of spilling in her mouth with each tug of her lips. Sanity was no longer an option with Sabrina. She had driven him toward a madness he welcomed with open arms.

Graham drew her up to his body and kissed her senseless. The essence of him melted on their tongues, making him crave a taste of her sweetness. He rolled her over and moved between her thighs, impatient to feed his hunger. Sabrina gripped his hair, urging him to her core.

With the first swipe of his tongue, Sabrina pressed herself into Graham's mouth. She rocked against him. His whiskers brushed across her thighs, bringing her to the height of ecstasy.

Each time his rough cheeks swiped across her thighs, she fed him with her wetness. He slid in two fingers, heightening her pleasure as he teased her clit with his tongue.

"Graham," his siren called out with her need.

However, Graham couldn't get enough of her. She was his salvation, and he had starved for her. He devoured her wetness with one lick after another, leaving her a trembling mess, begging for him before he slid his cock inside her.

Sabrina wrapped her limbs around Graham, climbing him as he brought their bodies to a fever pitch with each stroke. No matter how tight she clung to him, she couldn't get close enough. Their passion clung to each other and demanded to abandon every doubt and embrace their love.

A sense of calm he couldn't describe suddenly overtook Graham. His kiss softened, and his strokes inside Sabrina's body slowed. He slid a hand along her body in a gentle caress to calm her soul. His lips trailed a path along her neck, down to her breast. He palmed the globe, bringing it to his lips for a soothing kiss. He pulled the nipple between his lips and tenderly sucked on the berry. Sabrina softened underneath him, and a sigh whispered past her lips.

He swiped his thumb back and forth across her nipple, then tugged it between his lips again. He bit down, and Sabrina moaned.

"My siren's moans cause my heart to quicken."

"Why does my pirate torment me so?"

Graham pressed in deeper and stilled. Sabrina whimpered. "Because he enjoys the treasures he finds with each moan and he hopes to find more."

Sabrina arched her body and rotated her hips, drawing out his moan. "Then perhaps your siren needs to show her pirate where every treasure she has is located." Sabrina lifted

Graham's hand from her breast and raised it to her heart. "It is your for eternity, my pirate."

Graham lowered his head and kissed her chest, then he moved their hands to his chest. "As mine is yours, my siren."

Sabrina pressed her lips against his chest. She cupped his cheek and pulled him in for a kiss filled with sorrow, forgiveness, hope, and most of all, love.

Graham pressed deeper into Sabrina and brought them to the pinnacle of unity. They no longer drowned or needed to be anchored. They floated on the bliss of finding the love meant only for them. He pulled her into his embrace and held her tight. Graham slipped away into sleep. Sabrina heard his soft snores and smiled with contentment.

She had found her home.

Chapter Twenty-Four

G RAHAM RAN THROUGH THE hallway, chasing Sabrina. In
cach hallway, they left the darkness behind and the sun
shined down on them. Her laughter teased him to follow her.
She glanced over her shoulder, and her eyes shined her love.

He reached out, but she evaded his grasp. Setting off again,
he found her near the ledge again. While he thought it was a
dream instead of a nightmare, he was mistaken.

"Sabrina, come away," he begged.

She smiled at him, holding out her hand. He gripped it,
trying to pull her away. "Look," she whispered.

Below them was an ocean of water, and reflecting off the
waves were images of them with children. A boat sat near a
cave, rocking in the water.

Sabrina jumped before he could stop her, and they landed
with a splash and the laughter of her siren call. She swam away
from him toward the images. And the pirate followed the lure
of his siren on a grand adventure.

He opened his eyes after his dream faded away and found
Sabrina watching him with her hand curled under her head.
She smiled at him.

"You stayed."

"A siren cannot leave a pirate after he captures her heart. It is an unspoken code," Sabrina teased.

He pulled her into his embrace. "Is that so?"

Sabrina kissed him. "Yes. Does my pirate wish to keep me?"

"He never plans to let you go again," Graham swore.

"I am sorry."

Graham pressed his forehead to hers. "No. We will never apologize for how we feel. Only from this day forth we will share our fears with each other."

"I need to explain about DeVille."

Graham rolled her over. "There is no need. He already has. Ah, love, I wish I could have saved you sooner."

Sabrina pressed her finger against his lips. "It is behind us now. I am free and yours if you will have me."

Graham nuzzled her neck. "I will have you in many delightful ways."

Sabrina giggled. "You are incorrigible."

Graham laughed. "So my family tells me frequently."

"I met Mina."

Graham smiled. "So I heard."

"She is a doll. Also, she mentioned something you never expressed to me."

Graham stilled, and Sabrina wondered if she had overstepped. Perhaps she had misunderstood his niece. When Graham sighed and pulled away, getting off the bed, she bit at her bottom lip to keep the tears away. She had presumed too much. He didn't plan to marry her and only wanted her as his mistress.

Graham glanced over his shoulder, trying to dig the box out of his wardrobe before Sabrina burst into tears. He had bought the ring the day after they shared their first kiss. It was presumptuous of him, but he knew then that she was his soul mate and he wanted to spend a lifetime with her. He listened to her sniffles and cringed at his foolishness. He should've calmed her fears and then presented her with the ring.

"A while back, I met this mermaid who lured me with her siren call. I fell under her spell, and the next day I purchased a treasure to give to her," Graham began and smiled when his hand closed over the jeweler's box.

Sabrina frowned. "I thought pirates searched for treasure?"

Graham lowered to the floor and stuck the box under her billow of hair, covering her face. "What can I say? The treasure I seek is more in the form of carnal pleasure," Graham teased.

When he pulled her hair back, it was to see a flush of pink warming her skin. He flipped the lid open and listened to the melody of her gasp. "Will my siren do me the honor of sailing the seven seas on my pirate ship?"

Sabrina gasped at the beautiful setting of diamonds surrounded by a cluster of various colored stones. A mermaid's ring. "I feared Mrs. Potts heard a false rumor."

Graham laughed at Sabrina's tease. He pulled her into his arms and showed her how exactly the rumors were true. Graham spent the day drawing out her siren sighs and declaring his love. Her laughter warmed his soul. He had scoffed at his brother through the years of a soul mate, declaring he wouldn't fall victim to love. But all it took was one glance across a theatre and he had fallen victim to the most amazing feeling ever. It was impossible to erase the heartache from her years spent in terror, but he would show Sabrina a lifetime filled with love and happiness. She was his soul mate he would spend an eternity with.

Sabrina sighed into each kiss from Graham. She never imagined her infatuation with a stranger would lead her to a happily ever after. Graham stood for every quality she wished in a gallant hero. It still amazed her how he quieted her ravished soul with his smile. Each wish she had made since she met him came true today. Graham gave Sabrina hope with each gentle kiss. She no longer feared the stability he represented but embraced the security. Every memory of unhappiness vanished in the wind within his embrace. Her heart overflowed with her love for him. Sabrina grew excited to travel on a new journey filled with happiness alongside her pirate lord.

Fate intertwined their destiny with a soul mate's love.

.

Epilogue

S ABRINA FOLLOWED GRAHAM INTO his family's drawing room. A warm blush covered her cheeks from the day spent in each other's arms. Graham couldn't wait to lure her back to their bed and draw a blush across her entire body.

He whispered in her ear, "Your blush is very becoming, my siren."

"Hush, pirate. Before I embarrass myself in front of your family. Whatever will your mother think of me if I throw myself in your arms and devour your lips?" Sabrina teased.

"She will declare her happiness at my luck in capturing you," Graham teased her in return.

Her blush darkened, and Graham chuckled with delight, drawing his family's attention toward them.

"Uncle Gam brought the mermaid home," Mina squealed, running toward them.

Graham caught her and lifted her in his arms. He whispered in her ear, "I captured her on my pirate ship and proposed."

"Did she say yes?" Mina whispered back.

Sabrina smiled and held up her hand for Mina to see.

"Oh, how pretty," Mina said in awe.

Sabrina and Graham shared a look at her description and laughed. The word would forever suffer between them because of the simple description.

"The mermaid said yes," Mina announced to the rest of the family.

Everyone laughed and gathered around them, offering their congratulations. Graham's family welcomed her with open arms, and soon she found herself teasing Graham along with them. And her pirate reacted by pulling her into his arms and kissing her scandalously until his mother swatted him away.

As she settled in his embrace on the sofa and watched him with his family, his smile was infectious, and she enjoyed his exuberance for life. She glanced over at Dracott, and he nodded in understanding at her sense of awe. Her friend understood more than anyone how she had never experienced this feeling of a family, and she knew he would offer her support whenever she needed it. Her glance moved on to Ravencroft, and he tipped his glass in welcome. The animosity they held for one another, forgotten.

When her gaze landed on Reese, he held a smile of gratitude toward her. She tilted her head, and he mouthed, "Welcome to the family," to her.

Graham's mother surprised her the most. She sat on the other side of Sabrina and offered her countless motherly hugs of affection. In her search for vengeance, she had found a caring family who offered their love unconditionally.

The only way love should be.

Hello Lovely Readers,

I hope you've enjoyed the Fate of the Worthingtons Series. It was a thrill to write a thrilling, passionate series filled with each member of the Worthington family finding love. Also, I enjoyed bringing back some characters from my Matchmaking Madness Series. I'm already plotting my next series. If you haven't yet, don't forget to join my newsletter to keep up-to-date with my latest news.

Happy Reading,

Laura

"Thank you for reading The Siren's Gentleman. Gaining exposure as an independent author relies mostly on word-of-mouth, so if you have the time and inclination, please consider leaving a short review wherever you can."

Want to join my mailing list? Visit https://www.lauraabarnes.com/contact-newsletter today!

Desire other books to read by Laura A. Barnes

Enjoy these other historical romances:

<u>Fate of the Worthingtons Series</u>
The Tempting Minx
The Seductive Temptress
The Fiery Vixen
The Siren's Gentleman

<u>Matchmaking Madness Series:</u>
How the Lady Charmed the Marquess
How the Earl Fell for His Countess
How the Rake Tempted the Lady
How the Scot Stole the Bride
How the Lady Seduced the Viscount
How the Lord Married His Lady

Tricking the Scoundrels Series:
Whom Shall I Kiss... An Earl, A Marquess, or A Duke?
Whom Shall I Marry... An Earl or A Duke?
I Shall Love the Earl
The Scoundrel's Wager
The Forgiven Scoundrel

Romancing the Spies Series:
Rescued By the Captain
Rescued By the Spy
Rescued By the Scot

About Author Laura A. Barnes

International selling author Laura A. Barnes fell in love with writing in the second grade. After her first creative writing assignment, she knew what she wanted to become. Many years went by with Laura filling her head full of story ideas and some funny fish songs she wrote while fishing with her family. Thirty-seven years later, she made her dreams a reality. With her debut novel *Rescued By the Captain*, she has set out on the path she always dreamed about.

When not writing, Laura can be found devouring her favorite romance books. Laura is married to her own Prince Charming (who for some reason or another thinks the heroes in her books are about him) and they have three wonderful children and two sweet grandbabies. Besides her love of reading and writing, Laura loves to travel. With her passport stamped in England, Scotland, and Ireland; she hopes to add more countries to her list soon.

While Laura isn't very good on the social media front, she loves to hear from her readers. You can find her on the following platforms:

You can visit her at ***www.lauraabarnes.com*** to join her mailing list.

Website: https://www.lauraabarnes.com/

Amazon: https://amazon.com/author/lauraabarnes

Goodreads: https://www.goodreads.com/author/show/16332844.Laura_A_Barnes

Facebook: https://www.facebook.com/AuthorLauraA.Barnes/

Instagram: https://www.instagram.com/labarnesauthor/

Twitter: https://twitter.com/labarnesauthor

BookBub: https://www.bookbub.com/profile/laura-a-barnes

TikTok: https://www.tiktok.com/@labarnesauthor

Manufactured by Amazon.ca
Bolton, ON

31309547R00139